Gaius Valerius Catullus, Robinson Ellis

The Poems and Fragments of Catullus

Gaius Valerius Catullus, Robinson Ellis

The Poems and Fragments of Catullus

ISBN/EAN: 9783744765701

Printed in Europe, USA, Canada, Australia, Japan

Cover: Foto ©Andreas Hilbeck / pixelio.de

More available books at **www.hansebooks.com**

THE

POEMS AND FRAGMENTS

OF

CATULLUS.

THE

POEMS AND FRAGMENTS

OF

CATULLUS,

TRANSLATED IN THE METRES OF THE ORIGINAL

BY

ROBINSON ELLIS,

FELLOW OF TRINITY COLLEGE, OXFORD,
PROFESSOR OF LATIN IN UNIVERSITY COLLEGE, LONDON.

LONDON:

JOHN MURRAY, ALBEMARLE STREET.

1871.

LONDON :

BRADBURY, EVANS, AND CO., PRINTERS, WHITEFRIARS.

TO ALFRED TENNYSON.

b

PREFACE.

THE idea of translating Catullus in the original metres adopted by the poet himself was suggested to me many years ago by the admirable, though, in England, insufficiently known, version of Theodor Heyse (Berlin, 1855). My first attempts were modelled upon him, and were so unsuccessful that I dropt the idea for some time altogether. In 1868, the year following the publication of my larger critical edition * of Catullus, I again took up the experiment, and translated into English glyconics the first Hymen-aeal, *Collis o Heliconici.* Tennyson's Alcaics and Hendecasyllables had appeared in the interval, and had suggested to me the new principle on which I was to go to work. It was not sufficient to reproduce the ancient metres, unless the ancient quantity was reproduced also. Almost all the modern writers of classical metre had contented themselves with making an accented syllable long, an unaccented short ; the

---

* The translation follows this edition (Oxford, 1867), in the constitution of the text, as well as in the sectional division of the poems.

most familiar specimens of hexameter, Longfellow's *Evangeline* and Clough's *Bothie of Tober-na-Vuolich* and *Amours de Voyage* were written on this principle, and, as a rule, stopped there. They almost invariably disregarded position, perhaps the most important element of quantity. In the first line of *Evangeline*—

This is the forest primeval, the murmuring pines and the hemlocks,

there are no less than five violations of position, to say nothing of the shortening of a syllable so distinctly long as the *i* in *primeval.* Mr. Swinburne, in his Sapphics and Hendecasyllables, while writing on a manifestly artistic conception of those metres, and, in my judgment, proving their possibility for modern purposes by the superior rhythmical effect which a classically trained ear enabled him to make in handling them, neglects position as a rule, though his nice sense of metre leads him at times to observe it, and uniformly rejects any approach to the harsh combinations indulged in by other writers. The nearest approach to quantitative hexameters with which I am acquainted in modern English writers is the *Andromeda* of Mr. Kingsley, a poem which has produced little effect, but is interesting as a step to what may fairly be called a new development of the metre. For the experiments of the Elizabethan writers, Sir Philip Sidney and others, by that strange perversity which

so often dominates literature, were as decidedly un-
successful from an accentual, as the modern experi-
ments from a quantitative point of view. Sir Philip
Sidney has given in his *Arcadia* specimens of hexa-
meters, elegiacs, sapphics, asclepiads, anacreontics,
hendecasyllables. The following elegiacs will serve
as a sample.

> *Unto a caitif wretch, whom long affliction holdeth,*
>   *And now fully believ's help to bee quite perished ;*
> *Grant yet, grant yet a look, to the last moment of his anguish,*
>   *O you (alas so I finde) caus of his onely ruine :*
> *Dread not awhit (O goodly cruel) that pitie may enter*
>   *Into thy heart by the sight of this Epistle I send :*
> *And so refuse to behold of these strange wounds the recitall,*
>   *Lest it might m' allure home to thyself to return.*

In these the classical laws of position are most care-
fully observed ; every dactyl ending in a consonant is
followed by a word beginning with a vowel or *h*—
*afflĭctĭŏn holdeth, momēnt ŏf hĭs anguish, caūse ŏf hĭs
onely ; afflidion wasteth, moment of his dolour, cause of
his dreary*, would have been as impossible to Sir
Philip Sidney as *moērŏr tĕnebat, momēntă pĕr curae,
caūsă vĕl sola* in a Latin writer of hexameters. Simi-
larly where the dactyl is incided after the second
syllable, the third syllable beginning a new word, the
utmost care is taken that that word shall begin not
only with a syllable essentially short, but, when the
second syllable ends in a consonant, with a vowel :

ŏf thĭs ĕpistle, but not *ŏf thĭs dĭsaster*, still less *ŏf thĭs direction*. The other element of quantity is less rigidly defined; for (1) syllables strictly long, as *I*, *thy*, *so*, are allowed to be short; (2) syllables made long by the accent falling upon them are in some cases shortened, as *rŭīne, pĕrĭshĕd, crŭēl*; (3) syllables which the absence of the accent only allows to be long *in thesi*, are, in virtue of the classical laws of position, permitted to rank as long elsewhere—*momēnt of his, ŏf this epistle*. It needs little reflection to see that it is to one or other of these three peculiarities that the failure of the Elizabethan writers of classical metres must be ascribed. Pentameters like

> *Gratefulness, sweetness, holy love, hearty regard,*
> *That the delights of life shall be to him dolorous,*
> *And even in that love shall I reserve him a spite;*

sapphics like

> *Are then humane mindes privileg'd so meanly*
> *As that hateful death can abridg them of power*
> *With the vow of truth to record to all worlds*
> *That we bee her spoils ?*

hexameters like

> *Fīre nŏ līquor can cool : Neptūnĕ's reālm would not avail us.*
> *Nurs inwārd mălădiĕs, which have not scope to bee breath'd out.*
> *Oh nŏ nŏ, worthie shephērd, worth cān never enter a title;*

are too alien from ordinary pronunciation to please either an average reader or a classically trained

student. The same may be said of the translation
into English hexameters of the two first Eclogues of
Virgil, appended by William Webbe to his *Discourse
of English Poetrie* (1586, recently reprinted by Mr.
Arber). Here is his version of Ecl. I., 1—10.

MELIBAEUS.

Tityrus, happilie then lyste tumbling under a beech tree,
All in a fine oate pipe these sweete songs lustilie chaunting:
We, poore soules goe to wracke, and from these coastes be remoued,
And fro our pastures sweete: thou Tityr, at ease in a shade plott
Makst thicke groues to resound with songes of brave Amarillis.

TITYRUS.

O Melibaeus, he was no man, but a God who relceude me:
Euer he shalbe my God: from this same Sheepcot his alters
Neuer, a tender lambe shall want, with blood to bedew them.
This good gift did he giue, to my steeres thus freelie to wander,
And to my selfe (thou seest) on pipe to resound what I listed.

ib. 50—56.

Here no unwoonted foode shall grieue young theaues who be laded,
Nor the infections foule of neighbours flocke shall annoie them.
Happie olde man. In shaddowy bankes and coole prettie places,
Heere by the quainted floodes and springs most holie remaining.
Here, these quicksets fresh which lands seuer out fro thy neighbors
And greene willow rowes which Hiblae bees doo rejoice in,
Otf fine whistring noise, shall bring sweete sleepe to thy sences.

The following stanzas are from a Sapphic ode into
which Webbe translated, or as we should say, trans-

posed the fourth Eclogue of Spenser's *Sheepheardes Calendar.*

> *Say, behold did ye euer her Angelike face,*
> *Like to Phoebe fayre? or her heauenly hauour*
> *And the princelike grace that in her remaineth?*
> > *haue yee the like seene?*

> *Vnto that place Caliope dooth high her,*
> *Where my Goddesse shines: to the same the Muser*
> *After her with sweete Violines about them*
> > *cheerefully tracing.*

> *All ye Sheepheardes maides that about the greene dwell,*
> *Speede ye there to her grace, but among ye take heede*
> *All be Virgins pure that aproche to deck her,*
> > *dutie requireth.*

> *When ye shall present ye before her in place,*
> *See ye not your selues doo demeane too rudely:*
> *Bynd the fillets: and to be fine the waste gyrt*
> > *fast with a tawdryne.*

> *Bring the Pinckes therewith many Gelliflowres sweete,*
> *And the Cullambynes: let vs haue the Wynesops,*
> *With the Coronation that among the loue laddes*
> > *wontes to be worne much.*

> *Daffadowndillies all a long the ground strowe,*
> *And the Cowslyppe with a prety paunce let heere lye.*
> *Kyngcuppe and Lillies so beloude of all men*
> > *and the deluce flowre.*

There are many faults in these verses; over quaint-nesses of language, constructions impossible in English,

quantities of doubtful correctness, harsh elisions, for
Webbe has tried even elisions. Yet, if I may trust
my judgment, all of them can still be read with plea-
sure; the sapphics may almost be called a success.
This is even more true of metres, where these faults
are less perceptible or more easily avoided, for in-
stance, Asclepiads. Take the verses on solitariness,
Arcadia, B. II. fin.

> *O sweet woods, the delight ōf sŏlītāriness !*
> *O how much I do like your solitariness!*
> *Where man's mind hath a freed consideration*
> *Of goodness to receive lovely direction.*

or the hendecasyllables immediately preceding,

> *Reason tell me thy minde, if here be reason,*
> *In this strange violence, to make resistance,*
> *Where sweet graces erect the stately banner.*

It is obvious that a very little more trouble would
have converted these into very perfect and very
pleasing poems. Had Sir Philip Sidney written every
asclepiad on the model of *Where man's mind hath a
freed consideration,* every hendecasyllable like *Where
sweet graces erect the stately banner,* the adjustment of
accent and quantity thus attained might, I think, have
induced greater poets than he to make the experiment
on a larger scale. But neither he nor his contem-

poraries were permitted to grasp as a principle a
regularity which they sometimes secured by chance ;
nor, so far as I am aware, have the various revivals of
ancient metre in this country or Germany in any case
consistently carried out the *whole* theory, without
which the reproduction is partial, and cannot look
for a more than partial success.   Even the four
specimens given in the posthumous edition of Clough's
poems, two of them elegiac, one alcaic, one in
hexameters, though professedly constructed on a
quantitative basis, and, in one instance (*Trunks the
forest yielded, with gums ambrosial oozing, &c.*) com-
bining legitimate quantity (in which accent and
position are alike observed) with illegitimate (in
which position is observed, but accent disregarded)
into a not unpleasing rhythm, cannot be considered as
more than imperfect realizations of the true positional
principle.   Tennyson's three specimens are, at least
in English, still unique.   It is to be hoped that he
will not suffer them to remain so.   Systems of Gly-
conics and Asclepiads are, if I mistake not, easily
manageable, and are only thought foreign to the
genius of our language because they have never been
written on strict principles of art by a really great
master.

What, then, are the rules on which such rhythms
become possible?   They are, briefly, these :—(1) ac-
cented syllables, *as a general rule*, are long, though

some syllables which count as long need not be accented, as in

All that on earth's leas blooms, what blossoms Thessaly nursing,

blossoms, though only accented on the first syllable, counts for a spondee, the shortness of the second *o* being partly helped out by the two consonants which follow it; partly by the fact that the syllable is *in thesi;* (2) the laws of position are to be observed, according to the general rules of classical prosody : (*a*) dactyls terminating in a consonant like *beautiful, bounteous,* or ending in a double vowel or a diphthong like *all of you, surely may, come to thee,* must be followed by a word beginning with a vowel or *y* or *h ;* dactyls terminating in a vowel or *y,* like *slippery,* should be followed, except in rare cases, by words beginning with a consonant ; trochees, whether composed of one word or more, should, if ending in a consonant, be followed by a vowel, if ending in the vowel *a,* by a consonant, thus, *planted around* not *planted beneath, Aurora the sun's* not *Aurora a sun's* (see however, lxiv. 253), but *unto a wood, any again, sorry at all, you be amused.* (*b*) Syllables made up of a vowel followed by two or more consonants, each of which is distinctly heard in pronunciation, as *long, sins, part, band, waits, souls, ears, must, heart, bright, strength, end, and, rapt, hers, dealt,* mo*ment,* bo*soms,* an*swers,* moun*tains,* bea*rest,* tum*bling,* gi*ving,* com*ing*, harbour*ing*, diffi*cult*, immi*nent*, strata*gems*, utter*ance*, happi*est*, trem*bling*ly, can never rank as short, even if unaccented and followed by a vowel, *h* or *y*. Thus, to go back to Longfellow's line,

This is the forest primeval, the murmuring pines and the hemlocks,

for*ĕ*st, *murmurĭng*, *pines ănd the*, are all inadmissible. But where a vowel is followed by two consonants, one of which is unheard or only heard slightly, as in *acc*use, sh*all*, *ass*emble, *diss*emble, kind*ness*, com*pass*, *aff*ect, *app*ear, *ann*oy, or when the second or third consonant is a liquid, as in *betray, beslime, besmear, depress, dethrone, agree*, the vowel preceding is so much more short than long as to be regularly admissible as short, rarely admissible as long. On this principle I have allowed *disōrdĕrlў, tēnăntlĕss, heavĕnlў*, to rank as dactyls.

These rules are after all only an outline, and perhaps can never be made more. It will be observed that they are more negative than positive. The reason of this is not far to seek. The main difference between my verses and those of other contemporary writers— the one point on which I claim for myself the merit of novelty—is the strict observance throughout of the rules of position. But the strict observance of position is in effect the strict avoidance of unclassical collocations of syllables : it is almost wholly negative. To illustrate my meaning I will instance the poems written in pure iambics, the *Phaselus ille* and *Quis hoc potest uidere.* Heyse translates the first line of the former of these poems by

Die Galeotte, die ihr schauet, liebe Herrn,

and this would be a fair representation of a pure iambic line, according to the views of most German and most English writers. Yet not only is *Die* no short syllable, but *ihr*, itself long, is made more hopelessly long by preceding three consonants in *schauet*, just as the last syllable of *schauet*, although in itself short, loses its right to stand for a true short in being followed by the first consonant of *liebe.* My own translation,

The puny pinnace yonder you, my friends, discern,

whatever its defects, is at least a pretty exact representation of a pure iambic line. xxix. 6–8, are thus translated by Heyse :—

Und jener soll in Uebermuthes Ueberfluss
Von einem Bett zum andern in die Runde gehn ?

by me thus,

Shall he in o'er-assumption, o'er-repletion he,
Sedately saunter every dainty couch along?

The difference is purely negative ; I have bound myself to avoid certain positions forbidden by the laws of ancient prosody. To some I may seem to have lost in vigour by the process; yet I believe the sense of triumph over the difficulties of our language, the satisfaction of approaching in a novel and perceptibly felt manner one of those excellences which, as much as anything, contributes to the permanent charm of Catullus, his dainty versification, will more than compensate for any shortcomings which the difficulty of the task has made inevitable. The same may be said of the elaborately artificial poem to Camerius (c. lv.), and the almost unapproachable Attis (c. lxiii.). Here, at least half the interest lies in the varied turns of the metre; if these can be represented with anything like faithfulness, the gain in exactness of prosody is enough, in my judgment, to counterbalance the possible loss of freedom in expression.

There is another circumstance which tends to make modern rules of prosody necessarily negative. Quantity, in English revivals of ancient metre, depends not only on position, but on accent. But accent varies greatly in different words; *heavy level ever cometh any*, have the same accent as *empty evil either boometh penny;* but the first syllable in the former set of words is lighter than in the latter. Hence, though accented, they may, on occasion, be considered and used as short; as, on the same principle, *dolorous stratagem echoeth family*, usually dactyls, may, on occasion, become tribrachs. But how lay

down any positive rule in a matter necessarily so fluc-
tuating? We cannot. All we can do is to refuse
admission as short syllables to any heavier accented
syllable. Here, then, much must be left to individual
discretion. My translation of the Attis will best
show my own feeling in the matter. But I am fully
aware that in this respect I have fallen far short of
consistency. I have made *any* sometimes short,
more often long; *to*, usually short, is lengthened in
lxi. 26, lxvii. 19, lxviii. 143; *with* is similarly long,
though not followed by a consonant, in lxi. 36; *given*
is long in xxviii. 7, short in xi. 17, lxiv. 213; *are* is
short in lxvii. 14; and more generally many syllables
allowed to pass for short in the Attis are elsewhere
long. Nor have I scrupled to forsake the ancient
quantity in proper names; following Heyse, I have
made the first syllable of *Verona* short in xxxv. 3,
lxvii. 34, although it retains its proper quantity in
lxviii. 27. Again, *Pheneos* is a dactyl in lxviii. 111,
while *Satrachus* is an anapaest in xcv. 5. In many
of these instances I have acted consciously; if the
writers of Greece and Rome allowed many syllables
to be doubtful, and almost as a principle avoid per-
fect uniformity in the quantity of proper names, a
greater freedom may not unfairly be claimed by their
modern imitators. If Catullus could write *Pharsăliam
coeunt, Pharsālia regna frequentant*, similar license
may surely be extended to me. I believe, indeed,

that nothing in my translation is as violent as the double quantity just mentioned in Catullus; but if there is, I would remind my readers of Goethe's answer to the boy who told him he had been guilty of a hexameter with seven feet, and applying the remark to any seeming irregularities in my own translation would say, *Lass die Bestie stehen.*

It would not be difficult to swell this Preface by enlarging on the novelty of the attempt, and indirectly panegyrising my own undertaking. I doubt whether any real advantage would thus be gained. If I have merely produced an elaborate failure, however much I might expatiate on the principles which guided me, my work would be an elaborate failure still. I shall therefore say no more, and shall be contented if I please the, even in this classically trained country, too limited number of readers who can really hear with their ears—if, to use the borrowed language of a great poet, I succeed in making myself vocal to the intelligent alone.

CATULLUS.

I.

WHO shall take thee, the new, the dainty volume,
  Purfled glossily, fresh with ashy pumice?

You, Cornelius; you of old did hold them
  Something worthy, the petty witty nothings,

While you venture, alone of all Italians,   5
  Time's vast chronicle in three books to circle,
  Jove! how arduous, how divinely learned!

  Therefore welcome it, yours the little outcast,
  This slight volume. O yet, supreme awarder,
Virgin, save it in ages on for ever.   10

II.

SPARROW, favourite of my own beloved,
  Whom to play with, or in her arms to fondle,
  She delighteth, anon with hardy-pointed
Finger angrily doth provoke to bite her:

When my lady, a lovely star to long for,   5
  Bends her splendour awhile to tricksy frolic;
  Peradventure a careful heart beguiling,
Pardie, heavier ache perhaps to lighten;

Might I, like her, in happy play caressing
  Thee, my dolorous heart awhile deliver!   10

   .   .   .   .

  I would joy, as of old the maid rejoiced
  Racing fleetly, the golden apple eyeing,
Late-won loosener of the wary girdle.

III.

WEEP each heavenly Venus, all the Cupids,
Weep all men that have any grace about ye.
Dead the sparrow, in whom my love delighted,
The dear sparrow, in whom my love delighted.

Yea, most precious, above her eyes, she held him, 5
  Sweet, all honey: a bird that ever hail'd her
  Lady mistress, as hails the maid a mother.

  Nor would move from her arms away: but only
  Hopping round her, about her, hence or hither,
Piped his colloquy, piped to none beside her.   10

Now he wendeth along the mirky pathway,
Whence, they tell us, is hopeless all returning.

Evil on ye, the shades of evil Orcus,
  Shades all beauteous happy things devouring,
  Such a beauteous happy bird ye took him.   15

Ah! for pity; but ah! for him the sparrow,
  Our poor sparrow, on whom to think my lady's
Eyes do angrily redden all a-weeping.

IV.   ·

1.

THE puny pinnace yonder you, my friends, discern,
  Of every ship professes agilest to be.
  Nor yet a timber o'er the waves alertly flew
  She might not aim to pass it; oary-wing'd alike
  To fleet beyond them, or to scud beneath a sail.   5

Nor here presumes denial any stormy coast
  Of Adriatic or the Cyclad orbed isles,
  A Rhodos immemorial, or that icy Thrace,
  Propontis, or the gusty Pontic ocean-arm,

Whereon, a pinnace after, in the days of yore   10
  A leafy shaw she budded; oft Cytorus' height .
  With her did inly whisper airy colloquy.

2.

Amastris, you by Pontus, you, the box-clad hill
  Of high Cytorus, all, the pinnace owns, to both
  Was ever, is familiar; in the primal years   15
  She stood upon your hoary top, a baby tree,
  Within your haven early dipt a virgin oar:

To carry thence a master o'er the surly seas,
  A world of angry water, hail'd to left, to right
  The breeze of invitation, or precisely set   20
  The sheets together op'd to catch a kindly Jove.

Nor yet of any power whom the coasts adore
　　Was heard a vow to soothe them, all the weary way
　　From outer ocean unto glassy quiet here.

But all the past is over ; indolently now　　　　25
She rusts, a life in autumn, and her age devotes
To Castor and with him ador'd, the twin divine. `

V.

LIVING, Lesbia, we should e'en be loving.
Sour severity, tongue of eld maligning,
All be to us a penny's estimation.

Suns set only to rise again to-morrow.
We, when sets in a little hour the brief light,　　　5
Sleep one infinite age, a night for ever.

Thousand kisses, anon to these an hundred,
Thousand kisses again, another hundred,
Thousand give me again, another hundred.

Then once heedfully counted all the thousands,　　10
We'll uncount them as idly ; so we shall not
Know, nor traitorous eye shall envy, knowing
All those myriad happy many kisses.

VI.

BUT that, Flavius, hardly nice or honest
　　This thy folly, methinks Catullus also
　　E'en had known it, a whisper had betray'd thee.

Some she-malady, some unhealthy wanton,
　　Fires thee verily : thence the shy denial.　　　5

Least, you keep not a lonely night of anguish ;
    Quite too clamorous is that idly-feigning
    Couch, with wreaths, with a Syrian odour oozing ;
    Then that pillow alike at either utmost
    Verge deep-dinted asunder, all the trembling   10
    Play, the strenuous unsophistication ;
    All, O prodigal, all alike betray thee.

Why ? sides shrunken, a sullen hip disabled,
    Speak thee giddy, declare a misdemeanour.

So, whatever is yours to tell or ill or   15
    Good, confess it. A witty verse awaits thee
    And thy lady, to place ye both in heaven.

VII.

Ask me, Lesbia, what the sum delightful
Of thy kisses, enough to charm, to tire me ?

Multitudinous as the grains on even
Lybian sands aromatic of Cyrene ;

'Twixt Jove's oracle in the sandy desert   5
And where royally Battus old reposeth ;

Yea a company vast as in the silence
Stars which stealthily gaze on happy lovers ;

E'en so many the kisses I to kiss thee
Count, wild lover, enough to charm, to tire me ;   10

These no curious eye can wholly number,
Tongue of jealousy ne'er bewitch nor harm them.

VIII.

AH poor Catullus, learn to play the fool no more.
  Lost is the lost, thou know'st it, and the past is past.

Bright once the days and sunny shone the light on thee, .
  Still ever hasting where she led, the maid so fair,
  By me belov'd as maiden is belov'd no more.   5

  Was then enacting all the merry mirth wherein
  Thyself delighted, and the maid she said not nay.
Ah truly bright and sunny shone the days on thee.

Now she resigns thee ; child, do thou resign no less,
Nor follow her that flies thee, or to bide in woe   10
Consent, but harden all thy heart, resolve, endure.

Farewell, my love.   Catullus is resolv'd, endures,
  He will not ask for pity, will not importune.

But thou'lt be mourning thus to pine unask'd alway.
  O past retrieval faithless ! Ah what hours are thine ! 15
  When comes a likely wooer ? who protests thou'rt fair ?

  Who brooks to love thee ? who decrees to live thine
    own ?
  Whose kiss delights thee ? whose the lips that own thy
    bite ?

Yet, yet, Catullus, learn to bear, resolve, endure.

IX.

DEAR Veranius, you of all my comrades
  Worth, you only, a many goodly thousands,

Speak they truly that you your hearth revisit,
Brothers duteous, homely mother aged?

Yes, believe them.   O happy news, Catullus!   5

I shall see him alive, alive shall hear him,
   Tribes Iberian, uses, haunts, declaring

   As his wont is; on him my neck reclining
Kiss his flowery face, his eyes delightful.

Now, all men that have any mirth about you,   10
Know ye happier any, any blither?

X.

In the Forum as I was idly roaming
Varus took me a merry dame to visit.
She a lady, methought upon the moment,
Of some quality, not without refinement.

I.

So, arrived, in a trice we fell on endless   5
   Themes collòquial; how the fact, the falsehood
   With Bithynia, what the case about it,
   Had it helped me to profit or to money.

Then I told her a very truth; no atom
   There for company, praetor, hungry natives,   10
   Home might render a body aught the fatter:

Then our praetor a castaway, could hugely
   Mulct his company, had a taste to jeer them.

2.

Spoke another, ' Yet anyways, to bear you
   Men were ready, enough to grace a litter.   15
   They grow quantities, if report belies not.'
   Then supremely myself to flaunt before her,

I ' So thoroughly could not angry fortune
   Spite, I might not, afflicted in my province,
   Get erected a lusty eight to bear me.   20

But so scrubby the poor sedan, the batter'd
   Frame-work, nobody there nor here could ever
   Lift it, painfully neck to nick adjusting.'

3.

Quoth the lady, belike a lady wanton,
   ' Just for courtesy, lend me, dear Catullus,   25
   Those same nobodies. I the great Sarapis
   Go to visit awhile.'   Said I in answer,

' Thanks ; but, lady, for all my easy boasting,
   'Twas too summary ; there's a friend who knows me,
   Cinna Gaius, his the sturdy bearers.   30

' Mine or Cinna's, an inch alone divides us,
   I use Cinna's, as e'en my own possession.
   But you're really a bore, a very tiresome
   Dame unmannerly, thus to take me napping.'

XI.

FURIUS and Aurelius, O my comrades,
   Whether your Catullus attain to farthest
   Ind, the long shore lash'd by reverberating
          Surges Eoan ;

Hyrcan or luxurious horde Arabian,   5
Sacan or grim Parthian arrow-bearer,
Fields the rich Nile discolorates, a seven-fold
        River abounding ;
Whether o'er high Alps he afoot ascending
Track the long records of a mighty Cæsar,   10
Rhene, the Gauls' deep river, a lonely Britain
        Dismal in ocean ;
This, or aught else haply the gods determine,
Absolute, you, with me in all to part not ;
Bid my love greet, bear her a little errand,   15
        Scarcely of honour.
Say ' Live on yet, still given o'er to nameless
Lords, within one bosom, a many wooers,
Clasp'd, as unlov'd each, so in hourly change all
        Lewdly disabled.   20
' Think not henceforth, thou, to recal Catullus'
Love ; thy own sin slew it, as on the meadow's
Verge declines, ungently beneath the plough-share
        Stricken, a flower.'

XII.

MARRUCINIAN Asinius, hardly civil
   Left-hand practices o'er the merry wine-cup.
   Watch occasion, anon remove the napkin.
   Call this drollery?   Trust me, friend, it is not.
   'Tis most beastly, a trick among a thousand.   5

Not believe me ? believe a friendly brother,
   Laughing Pollio ; he declares a talent
   Poor indemnification, he the parlous
   Child of voluble humour and facetious.

So face hendecasyllables, a thousand,   10
    Or most speedily send me back the napkin ;
    Gift not prized at a sorry valuation,
    But for company ; 'twas a friend's memento.

Cloth of Saetabis, exquisite, from utmost
    Iber, sent as a gift to me Fabullus   15
    And Veranius.   Ought not I to love them
    As Veranius even, as Fabullus ?

XIII.

PLEASE kind heaven, in happy time, Fabullus,
    We'll dine merrily, dear my friend, together.

Promise only to bring, your own, a dinner
    Rich and goodly ; withal a lily maiden,
    Wine, and banter, a world of hearty laughing.   5

Promise only ; betimes we dine, my gentle
    Friend, most merrily ; but, for your Catullus—
    Know he boasts but a pouch of empty cobwebs.

Yet take contrary fee, the quintessential
    Love, or sweeter if aught is, aught supremer,   10

Perfume savoury, mine ; my love received it
Gift of every Venus, all the Cupids.

Would you smell it ? a god shall hear Fabullus
Pray unbody him only nose for ever.

XIV.

CALVUS, save that as eyes thou art beloved,
  I could verily loathe thee for the morning's
  Gift, Vatinius hardly more devoutly.

Slain with poetry ! done to death with abjects !
  O what syllable earn'd it, act allow'd it ?   5
  Gods, your malison on the sorry client
Sent that rascally rabble of malignants.

Yet, if, freely to guess, the gift recherché
  Some grammarian, haply Sulla, sent thee ;
  I repine not ; a dear delight, a triumph   10
This, thy drudgery thus to see rewarded.

Gods ! an horrible and a deadly volume !

Sent so faithfully, friend, to thy Catullus,
  Just to kill him upon a day, the festive,
  Saturnalia, best of all the season.   15
Sure, a drollery not without requital.

For, come dawn, to the cases and the bookshops
  I ; there gather a Caesius and Aquinus,
  With Suffenus, in every wretch a poison :
Such plague-prodigy thy remuneration !   20

Now good-morrow ! away with evil omen
  Whence ill destiny lamely bore ye, clumsy
  Poet-rabble, an age's execration !

XIV B.

Readers, any that in the future ever
Scan my fantasies, haply lay upon me
Hands adventurous of solicitation—

XV.

LEND thy bounty to me, to my beloved,
   Kind Aurelius.   I do ask a favour

   Fair and lawful ; if you did e'er in earnest
   Seek some virginal innocence to cherish,
Touch not lewdly the mistress of my passion.   5

Trust the people ; avails not aught to fear them,
   Such, who hourly within the streets repassing,
   Run, good souls, on a busy quest or idle.

You, you only the free, the felon-hearted,
   Fright me, prodigal you of every virtue.   10

   Well, let luxury run her heady riot,
   Love flow over ; enough abroad to sate thee :
This one trespass—a tiny boon—presume not.

But should impious heat or humour headstrong
   Drive thee wilfully, wretch, to such profaning,   15
   In one folly to dare a double outrage :

Ah what misery thine ; what angry fortune !
   Heels drawn tight to the stretch shall open inward
   Lodgment easy to mullet and to radish.

XVI.

I'LL traduce you, accuse you, and abuse you,
 Soft Aurelius, e'en as easy Furius.
 You that lightly a saucy verse resenting,
Misconceit me, sophisticate me wanton.

Know, pure chastity rules the godly poet,   ·   5
 Rules not poesy, needs not e'er to rule it ;
 Charms some verse with a witty grace delightful ?
'Tis voluptuous, impudent, a wanton.

It shall kindle an icy thought to courage,
 Not boy-fancies alone, but every frozen   10
 Flank immovable, all amort to pleasure.

You my kisses, a million happy kisses,
 Musing, read me a silky thrall to softness?
I'll traduce you, accuse you, and abuse you.

XVII.

I.

KIND Colonia, fain upon bridge more lengthy to gambol,
 And quite ready to dance amain, fearing only the rotten
· Legs too crazily steadied on planks of old resurrections,
 Lest it plunge to the deep morass, there supinely to
  welter ;
So surprise thee a sumptuous bridge thy fancy to plea-
  sure,   5
Passive under a Salian god's most lusty procession ;
This rare favour, a laugh for all time, Colonia, grant me.

In my township a citizen lives : Catullus adjures thee
  Headlong into the mire below topsy-turvy to drown him.
  Only, where the superfluent lake, the spongy putres-
      cence,   10
  Sinks most murkily flushed, descends most profoundly
      the bottom.

Such a ninny, a fool is he ; witless even as any
  Two years' urchin, across papa's elbow drowsily
    . swaying.

2.

For though wed to a maiden in spring-tide youthfully
    budding,
  Maiden crisp as a petulant kid, as airily wanton,   15
  Sweets more privy to guard than e'er grape-bunch
      shadowy-purpling ;
  He, he leaves her alone to romp idly, cares not a fouter.
  Nor leans to her at all, the man's part ; but helpless as
      alder
  Lies, new-fell'd in a ditch, beneath axe Ligurian ham-
      strung,
  As alive to the world, as if world nor wife were at issue. 20

Such this gaby, my own, my arch fool ; he sees not, he
    hears not
  Who himself is, or if the self is, or is not, he knows not.

  Him I'd gladly be lowering down thy bridge to the
      bottom,
  If from stupor inanimate peradventure he wake him,
Leaving muddy behind him his sluggish heart's hesita-
      tion,   25
  As some mule in a glutinous sludge her rondel of iron.

XXI.

SIRE and prince-patriarch of hungry starvelings,
  Lean Aurelius, all that are, that have been,
  That shall ever in after years be famish'd ;

  Wouldst thou lewdly my dainty love to folly
  Tempt, and visibly? thou be near, be joking   5
Cling and fondle, a hundred arts redouble?

O presume not : a wily wit defeated
  Pays in scandalous incapacitation.

Yet didst folly to fulness add, 'twere all one ;
  Now shall beauty to thirst be train'd or hunger's 10
Grim necessity ; this is all my sorrow.

Then hold, wanton, upon the verge ; to-morrow
Comes preposterous incapacitation.

XXII.

SUFFENUS, he, dear Varus, whom, methinks, you know,
  Has sense, a ready tongue to talk, a wit urbane,
  And writes a world of verses, on my life no less.

Ten times a thousand he, believe me, ten or more,
  Keeps fairly written ; not on any palimpsest,   5
  As often, enter'd, paper extra-fine, sheets new,
  New every roller, red the strings, the parchment-case
Lead-rul'd, with even pumice all alike complete.

You read them : our choice spirit, our refin'd rare wit,
  Suffenus, O no ditcher e'er appeared more rude,   10
  No looby coarser ; such a shock, a change is there.

How then resolve this puzzle? He the birthday-wit,
  For so we thought him—keener yet, if aught is so—
  Becomes a dunce more boorish e'en than hedge-
      born boor,
  If e'er he faults on verses; yet in heart is then   15
  Most happy, writing verses, happy past compare,
  So sweet his own self, such a world at home finds he.

Friend, 'tis the common error; all alike are wrong,
Not one, but in some trifle you shall eye him true
Suffenus; each man bears from heaven the fault they
      send,   20
None sees within the wallet hung behind, our own.

XXIII.

NEEDY Furius, house nor hoard possessing,
  Bug or spider, or any fire to thaw you,
  Yet most blest in a father and a step-dame,
  Each for penury fit to tooth a flint-stone:
  Is not happiness yours? a home united?   5
  Son, sire, mother, a lathy dame to match him.

Who can wonder? in all is health, digestion,
  Pure and vigorous, hours without a trouble.
  Fires ye fear not, or house's heavy downfal,
  Deeds unnatural, art in act to poison,   10
  Dangers myriad accidents befalling.

Then your bodies? in every limb a shrivell'd
  Horn, all dryness in all the world whatever,
  Tann'd or frozen or icy-lean with ages.
  Sure superlative happiness surrounds thee.   15

Thee sweat frets not, an o'er-saliva frets not,
Frets not snivel or oozy rheumy nostril.

Yet such purity lacks not e'en a purer.
   White those haunches as any cleanly-silver'd
   Salt, it takes you a month to barely dirt them.   20
   Then like beans, or inert as e'er a pebble,
   Those impeccable heavy loins, a finger's
Breadth from apathy ne'er seduced to riot.

Such prosperity, such superb profusion,
Slight not, Furius, idly nor reject not.   25
As for sesterces, all the would-be fortune,
Cease to wish it ; enough, methinks, the present.

XXIV.

O THOU blossom of all the race Juventian
   Not now only, but all as yet arisen,
   All to flower in after-years arising ;

   Midas' treasury better you presented
   Him that owns not a slave nor any coffer,   5
Ere you suffer his alien arm's presuming.

What? you fancy him all refin'd perfection?
   Perfect! truly, without a slave, a coffer.

Slight, reject it, away with it ; for all that
   He, he owns not a slave nor any coffer.   10

XXV.

SMOOTH Thallus, inly softer you than any furry rabbit,
   Or glossy goose's oily plumes, or velvet earlap yielding,
   Or feeble age's heavy thighs, or flimsy filthy cobweb ;

And Thallus, hungry rascal you, as hurricane rapacious,
When winks occasion on the stroke, the gulls agape
declaring :   5

Return the mantle home to me, you watch'd your hour
to pilfer,
The fleecy napkin and the rings from Thynia quaintly
graven,
Whatever you parade as yours, vain fool, a sham rever-
sion :

Unglue the nails adroit to steal, unclench the spoil, deliver,
Lest yet that haunch voluptuous, those tender hands
caressant,   10
Should take an ugly print severe, the scourge's heavy
branding ;
And strange to bruises you should heave, as heaves in
open Ocean,
Some little hoy surprised adrift, when wails the windy
water.

XXVI.

DRAUGHTS, dear Furius, if my villa faces,
'Tis not showery south, nor airy wester,
North's grim fury, nor east ; 'tis only fifteen
Thousand sesterces, add two hundred over.
Draft unspeakable, icy, pestilential !   5

XXVII.

Boy, young caterer of Falernian olden,
Brim me cups of a fiercer harsher essence ;
So Postumia, queen of healths presiding,
Bids, less thirsty the thirsty grape, the toper.

But dull water, avaunt.   Away the wine-cup's   5
Sullen enemy ; seek the sour, the solemn !
Here Thyonius hails his own elixir.

XXVIII.

STARVING company, troop of hungry Piso,
  Light of luggage, of outfit expeditious,
  You, Veranius, you, my own Fabullus,

Say, what fortune ? enough of empty masters,
Frost and famine, a lingering probation?   5

Stands your diary fair ? is any profit
  Enter'd *given ?* as I to serve a praetor
  Count each beggarly gift a timely profit.

Trust me, Memmius, you did aptly finger
My passivity, fool'd me most supinely.   10

Friends, confess it ; in e'en as hard a fortune
  You stand mulcted, on you a like abashless
  Rake rides heavily.   Court the great who wills it !

Gods and goddesses evil heap upon ye,
Rogues to Romulus and to Remus outcast.   15

XXIX.

CAN any brook to see it, any tamely bear—
  If any, gamester, epicure, a wanton, he—
  Mamurra's own whatever all the curly Gauls
  Did else inherit, or the lonely Briton isle ?
Can you look on, look idly, filthy Romulus?   5

Shall he, in o'er-assumption, o'er-repletion he,
  Sedately saunter every dainty couch along,

A bright Adonis, as the snowy dove serene?
Can you look on, look idly, filthy Romulus?
Look idly, gamester, epicure, a wanton, you.   10

Unique commander, and was only this the plea
    Detain'd you in that islet angle of the west,
    To gorge the shrunk seducer irreclaimable
    With haply twice a million, add a million yet?
What else was e'er unhealthy prodigality?   15

The waste? to lust a little? on the belly less?
    Begin; a glutted hoard paternal; ebb the first.
    To this, the booty Pontic; add the spoil from out
    Iberia, known to Tagus' amber ory stream.
Not only Gaul, nor only quail the Briton isles.   20

What help a rogue to fondle? is not all his act
    To swallow monies, empty purses heap on heap?
    But you—to please him only, shame to Rome, to me!
    Could you the son, the father, idly ruin all?

XXX.

FALSE Alfenus, in all amity frail, duty a prodigal,
Doth thy pity depart? Shall not a friend, traitor, a friend
    recal

Love? what courage is here me to betray, me to re-
    pudiate?

.   .   .   .
.   .' .   .   .   .   .   , ... 5
Never sure did a lie, never a sin, please the celestials.

This you heed not; alas! leave me to new misery, deso-
    late.   (5)
O where now shall a man trust? liveth yet any fidelity?

You, you only did urge love to be free, life to surrender, you.
Guiding into the snare, falsely secure, prophet of happi-
 ness.   10

Now you leave me, retract, every deed, every word allow
Into nullity winds far to remove, vapoury clouds to
 bear.   (10)

You forget me, but yet surely the Gods, surely remem-
 bereth
Faith ; hereafter again honour awakes, causeth a wretch
 to rue.

XXXI.

O THOU of islands jewel and of half-islands,
 Fair Sirmio, whatever o'er the lakes' clear rim
 Or waste of ocean, Neptune holds, a two-fold pow'r ;
What joy have I to see thee, and to gaze what glee !

Scarce yet believing Thunia past, the fair champaign   5
 Bithunian, yet in safety thee to greet once more.
 From cares to part us—where is any joy like this ?

Then drops the soul her fardel, as the travel-tir'd
 World-weary wand'rer touches home, returns, sinks
  down
 In joy to slumber on the bed desir'd so long.   ·10
This meed, this only counts for e'en an age all toil.

O take a welcome, lovely Sirmio, thy lord's,
 And greet him happy ; greet him all the lake Lydian ;
 Laugh out whatever laughter at the hearth rings clear.

XXXII.

LIST, I charge thee, my gentle Ipsithilla,
Lovely ravisher and my dainty mistress,
Say we'll linger a lazy noon together.

Suits my company? lend a farther hearing:
See no jealousy make the gate against me,   5
See no fantasy lead thee out a-roaming.
Keep close chamber; anon in all profusion
Count me kisses again again returning.

Bides thy will? with a sudden haste command me;
Full and wistful, at ease reclin'd, a lover   10
Here I languish alone, supinely dreaming.

XXXIII.

MASTER-robber of all that haunt the bath-rooms,
Old Vibennius, and his heir the wanton;
(His the dirtier hands, the greedy father,
Yours the filthier heart, his heir as hungry;)

Please your knaveries hoist a sail for exile,   5
Pains and privacy? since by this the father's
Thefts are palpable, and a rusty favour,
Son, picks never a penny from the people.

XXXIV.

GREAT Diana protecteth us,
Maids and boyhood in innocence.
Maidens virtuous, innocent
          Boys, your song be Diana.

Hail, Latonia, thou that art   5
Throned daughter of enthronis'd
Jove ; near Delian olive of
      Mighty mother y-boren.
Queen of mountainous heights, of all
Forests leafy, delightable ;   10
Glens in bowery depths remote,
      Rivers wrathfully sounding.
Thee, Lucina, the travailing
Mother haileth, a sovereign
Juno ; Trivia thou, the bright   15
      Moon, a glory reflected.
Thou thine annual orb anew,
Goddess, monthly remeasuring,
Farmsteads lowly with affluent
      Corn dost fill to the flowing.   20
Be thy heavenly name whate'er
Name shall please thee, in hallowing ;
Still keep safely the glorious
      Race of Romulus olden.

XXXV.

1.

TAKE Caecilius, him the tender-hearted
  Bard, my paper, a wish from his Catullus.
  Come from Larius, haste to leave the new-built
Comum's watery city, seek Verona.

Some particular intimate reflexions   5
One would tell thee, a friend we love together.

2.

So he'll quickly devour the way, if only
  He's no booby ; for all a snowy maiden

Chide imperious, and her hands around him
Both in jealousy clasp'd, refuse departure.　　　10

She, if only report the truth bely not,
Doats, as hardly within her own possession.

3.

For since lately she read his high-preluding
Queen of Dindymus, all her heart is ever
Melting inly with ardour and with anguish.　　　15

Maiden, laudable is that high emotion,
Muse more rapturous, you, than any Sappho.
The Great Mother he surely sings divinely.

XXXVI.
1.

VILEST paper of all dishonour, annals
Of Volusius, hear my lovely lady's

Vow, and pay it ; awhile she swore to Venus
And fond Cupid, if ever I returning
Ceased from enmity, left to launch iambics,　　　5

She would surely devote the sorry poet's
Choicest rarities unto sooty Vulcan,
The lame deity, there to blaze lamenting.

With such drollery, such supreme defiance,
Swore strange oath to the gods the naughty wanton. 10

2.

Now, O heavenly child of azure Ocean,
Queen of Idaly, queen of Urian highlands,

Who Ancona the fair, the reedy Cnidos
Hauntest, Amathus and the lawny Golgi,
Or Dyrrhachium, hostel Adriatic ;　　　15

Hear thy votaress, answer her petition ;
  'Tis most graceful, a dainty thought to charm thee.

But ye verses, away to fire, to burning,
  Rank rusticities, empty vapid annals
  Of Volusius, heap of all dishonour.   20

XXXVII.

I.

O FROWSY tavern, frowsy fellowship therein,
  Ninth post in order next beyond the twins cap-crown'd,

Shall manly service none but you alone employ,
  Shall you alone whatever in the world smiles fair,
  Possess it, every other hold to lack esteem ?   5

Or if in idiot impotence arow you sit,
  One hundred, yes two hundred, am not I, think you,
  A man to þring mine action on your whole row there ?

So think not, he that likes not ; answer how you may,
  With scorpion I, with emblem all your haunt will
      scrawl.   10

2.

For she the bright one, lately fled beyond these arms,
  The maid belov'd as maiden is belov'd no more,
  Whom I to win, stood often in the breach, fought long,

Has sat amongst you.   Her the grand, the great, all, all
  Do dearly love her; yea, beshrew the damned wrong, 15
  Each slight seducer, every lounger highway-born,

You chiefly, peerless paragon of the.tribe long-lock'd,
  Rude Celtiberia's child, the bushy rabbit-den,

Egnatius, so modish in the big bush-beard,
  And teeth a native lotion hardly scours quite pure.   20

XXXVIII.

CORNIFICIUS, ill is your Catullus,
  Ill, ah heaven, a weary weight of anguish,
  More more weary with every day, with each hour.

You deny me the least, the very lightest
  Help, one whisper of happy thought to cheer me.   5

Nay, I'm sorrowful. You to slight my passion?
  Ah! one word, but a tiny word to cheer me,
  Sad as ever a tear Simonidean.

XXXIX.

1.

EGNATIUS, spruce owner of superb white teeth,
  Smiles sweetly, smiles for ever: is the bench in view
  Where stands a pleader just prepar'd to rouse our tears,

Egnatius smiles sweetly; near the pyre they mourn
  Where weeps a mother o'er the lost, the kind one son, 5
  Egnatius smiles sweetly; what the time or place

Or thing soe'er, smiles sweetly; such a rare complaint
Is his, not handsome, scarce to please the town, say I.

2.

So take a warning for the nonce, my friend; town-bred
  Were you, a Sabine hale, a pearly Tiburtine,   10
  A frugal Umbrian body, Tuscan huge of paunch,

A grim Lanuvian black of hue, prodigious-tooth'd,
  A Transpadane, my country not to pass untax'd,
  In short whoever cleanly cares to rinse foul teeth,

Yet sweetly smiling ever I would have you not, 15
 For silly laughter, it's a silly thing indeed.

3.

Well: you're a Celtiberian ; in the parts thereby
 What pass'd the night in water, every man, come dawn,
 Scours clean the foul teeth with it and the gums rose-
 red ;

So those Iberian snowy teeth, the more they shine, 20
 So much the deeper they proclaim the draught impure.

XL.

WHAT fatality, what chimera drives thee
 Headlong, Ravidus, on to my iambics ?

What fell deity, most malign to listen,
 Fires thy fury to quarrel unavailing ?

Wouldst thou busy the breath of half the people ? 5
 Break with clamour at any cost the silence ?

Thou wilt do it ; a wretch that hop'd my darling
 Love to fondle, a sure retaliation.

XLI.

AMEANA, the maiden of the people,
 Asks me sesterces, all the many thousands.

Maiden she with a nose not wholly faultless,
 Bankrupt Formian, your declar'd devotion.

Wherefore look to the maiden, her relations: 5
 Call her family, summon all the doctors.

Your poor maiden is oddly touch'd ; a mirror
 Sure would lend her a soberer reflexion.

XLII.

1.

COME all hendecasyllables whatever,
  Wheresoever ye house you, all whatever.

I the game of an impudent adultress?
  She refuse to return to me the tablets
  Where you syllable?   O ye can't be silent.   5
Up, have after her, ask renunciation.

Would ye know her? a woman, you shall eye her
  Strutting loftily, whiles she laughs a loud laugh
  Vast and vulgar, a Gaulish hound beseeming.
Form your circle about her, ask her, urge her.   10

' Hark, adulteress, hand the note-book over.
  Hark, the note-book, adultress, hand it over.'

2.

What? you scorn us?   O ugly filth, detested
  Trull, whatever is all abomination.

Nay then, louder.   Enough as yet it is not.   15
  If this only remains, perhaps the dog-like
  Face may colour, a brassy blush may yield us.
  Swell your voices in higher harsher yellings,

' Hark, adulteress, hand the note-book over;
  Hark, the note-book; adultress, hand it over.'   20

Look, she moves not at all: we waste the moments.
  Change your quality, try another issue.
  Such composure a sweeter air may alter.
' Pure and virtuous, hand the note-book over.'

XLIII.

HAIL, fair virgin, a nose among the larger, ·
    Feet not dainty, nor eyes to match a raven,
    Mouth scarce tenible, hands not wholly faultless,
    Tongue most surely not absolute refinement,
Bankrupt Formian, your declar'd devotion.   5
    Thou the beauty, the talk of all the province?
    Thou my Lesbia tamely think to rival?
O preposterous, empty generation!

XLIV.

O THOU my Sabine farmstead or my Tiburtine,
    For who Catullus would not harm, avow, kind souls,
    Thou surely art at Tibur; and who quarrel will
Sabine declare thee, stake the world to prove their say:

But be'st a Sabine, be'st a very Tiburtine,   5
    At thy suburban villa what delight I knew
    To spit the tiresome cough away, my lungs' ill guest,
    My belly brought me, not without a sad weak sin,
Because a costly dinner I desir'd too much.

For I, to feast with Sestius, that host unmatch'd,   10
A speech of his, pure poison, every line deep-drugg'd,
His speech against the plaintiff Antius, read through.

Whereat a cold chill, soon a gusty cough in fits,
    Shook, shook me ever, till to thy retreat I fled,
    There duly dosed with nettle and repose found cure. 15
    So, now recruited, thanks superlative, dear farm,
I give thee, who so lightly didst avenge that sin.

And trust me, farm, if ever I again take up
  With Sextius' black charges, I'll rebel no more ;
   But let the chill things damn to cold, to cough, not me 20
That read the volume—no, but him, the man's vain self.

XLV.

I.

WHILE Septimius in his arms his Acme
  Fondled closely, 'My own,' said he, ' my Acme,

  If I love not as unto death, nor hold me
  Ever faithfully well-prepar'd to largest
  Strain of fiery wooer yet to love thee,   5

  Then in Libya, then may I alone in
  Burning India face a sulky lion.'

Scarce he ended, upon the right did eager
  Love sneeze amity ; 'twas before to leftward.

2.

Acme quietly back her head reclining   10
  Towards her boy, with a rosy mouth delightful
  Kissed his passionate eyes elately swimming,

  Then 'Septimius, O my life' she murmur'd,
  ' So may he that is in this hour ascendant

  Rule us ever, as in me burns a greater   15
  Fire, a fiercer, in every vein triumphing.'

Scarce she ended, upon the right did eager
  Love sneeze amity ; 'twas before to leftward.

3.

So, that augury joyous each possessing,
Loves, is lov'd with an even emulation.   20

Poor Septimius, all to please his Acme,
Recks not Syria, recks not any Britain.

In Septimius only faithful Acme
Makes her softnesses, holds her happy pleasures.

When did mortal on any so rejoicing   25
Look, on union hallow'd as divinely?

XLVI.

Now soft spring with her early warmth returneth,
  Now doth Zephyrus, health benignly breathing,
  Still the boisterous equinoctial heaven.

Leave we Phrygia, leave the plains, Catullus,
  Leave Nicaea, the sultry soil of harvest: 5
On for Asia, for the starry cities.
  Now all flurry the soul is out a-ranging,
Now with vigour aflame the feet renew them.

Farewell company true, my lovely comrades.
  You so joyfully borne from home together,   10
  Now o'er many a weary way returning.

XLVII.

Porcius, Socration, the greedy Piso's
  Tools of thievery, rogues to famish ages,

So that filthy Priapus ousts to please you
  My Veranius even and Fabullus?

What? shall you then at early noon carousing   5
  Lap in luxury? they, my jolly comrades,
  Search the streets on a quest of invitation?

XLVIII.

IF, Juventius, I the grace win ever
  Still on beauteous honied eyes to kiss thee,
  I would kiss them a million, yet a million.

Yea, nor count me to win the full attainment,
  Not, tho' heavier e'en than ears at harvest,   5
  Fall my kisses, a wealthy crop delightful.

XLIX.

GREATEST speaker of any born a Roman,
  Marcus Tullius, all that are, that have been,
  That shall ever in after-years be famous ;

Thanks superlative unto thee Catullus
  Renders, easily last among the poets.   5

He as easily last among the poets
  As thou surely the first among the pleaders.

L.

1.

DEAR Lucinius, yestereve we linger'd
  Scrawling fancies, a hundred, in my tablets,
  Wits in combat ; a treaty this between us.

Scribbling drolleries each of us together
  Launched one arrowy metre and another,   5
  Tenders jocular o'er the merry wine-cup.

2.

So quite sorely with all your humour heated
  Gay Lucinius, I that eve departed.

Food my misery could not any lighten,
  Sleep nor quiet upon my eyes descended.   10

Still untamable o'er the couch did I then
  Turn and tumble, in haste to see the day-light,
  Hear your prattle again, again be with you.

3.

Then, when weary with all the worry, numb'd, dead,
  Sank my body, upon the bed reposing,   15
  This, O humorous heart, did I, a poem
  Write, my tedious anguish all revealing.

O beware then of hardihood ; a lover's
  Plea for charity, dear my friend, reject not :
  What if Nemesis haply claim repayment ?   20
  She is tyrannous.   O beware offending.

LI.

HE to me like unto the Gods appeareth,
· He, if I dare speak it, ascends above them,
Face to face who toward thee attently sitting
      Gazes or hears thee
Lovely in sweet laughter ; alas within me   5
Every lost sense falleth away for anguish ;
When as I look'd on thee, upon my lips no
      Whisper abideth,
Straight my tongue froze, Lesbia ; soon a subtle
· Fire thro' each limb streameth adown; with inward 10
Sound the full ears tinkle, on either eye night's
      Canopy darkens.
Ease alone, Catullus, alone afflicts thee ;

                  D

Ease alone breeds error of heady riot ;
Ease hath entomb'd princes of old renown and   15
     Cities of honour.

LII.

ENOUGH, Catullus ! how can you delay to die ?
   If in the curule chair a hump sits, Nonius ;
   A would-be consul lies in hope, Vatinius ;
Enough, Catullus ! how can you delay to die ?

LIII.

HOW I laughed at a wag amid the circle !
   He, when Calvus in high denunciation
   Of Vatinius had declaim'd divinely,
   Hands uplifted as in supreme amazement,
Cried 'God bless us ! a wordy cockalorum!'   5

LIV.

OTHO'S head is a very dwarf; a rustic's
   Shanks has Herius, only semi-cleanly ;
   Libo's airs to a fume of art refine them.

. . . .

. . . .   5

Yet thou flee'st not above my keen iambics.

. . . .

. . . .

[So may destiny doom me quite to silence]
As I care not if every line offend thee   10
And Sufficius, age in youth's revival.

. . . .

Thou shalt kindle at innocent iambics,
Mighty general, once again returning.

LV.

1.

List, I beg, provided you're in humour,
　Speak your privacy, show what alley veils you.
You I sought on Campus, I, the lesser,
　You on Circus, in all the bills but you, sir.
You with father Jove in holy temple. 5
　Then, where flocks the parade to Magnus' arches,

　　Friend, I hail'd each lady promenader,
　　Each, I found, did face me quite sedately.

2.

What? they steal, I loudly cried protesting,
　My Camerius? out upon the wenches ! 10
Answer'd one and lightly bared a bosom,
　' See ! what bowery roses ; here he hides him.'

　　Yea 'twould task e'en Hercules to bear you,
　　You so scornful, friend, in your refusing.

3.

Not tho' I were warder of the Cretans, 15
　Not tho' Pegasus on his airy pinion,

　　Perseus feathery-footed, I a Ladas,
　　Rhesus' chariot yok'd to snowy coursers,
　　Add each feathery sandal, every flying
　　Power, ask fleetness of all the winds of heaven, 20
　　Mine, Camerius, and to me devoted ;
　　Yet with drudgery sorely spent should I, yet

　Worn, outworn with languor unto languor
　　Faint, O friend, in an empty quest to find you.

4.

Say, where think you anon to be ; declare it, 25 (15)
    Fair and free, submit, commit to daylight.
What ? still thrall to the lovely lily ladies ?
    Keep close mouth, lock fast the tongue within it,
Love's felicity falls without fruition :
    Venus still is free to talk, a babbler.   30 (20)
Yet close palate, an if ye will it ; only
    In my love some part to bear refuse not.

LVII.

O RARE sympathies ! happy rakes united !
    There Mamurra the woman, here a Caesar.

Who can wonder?   An ugly brand on either,
    His, true Formian, his, politely Roman,
    Rests indelible, in the bone residing.   5

Either infamous, each a twin dishonour,
    Bookish brethren, a dainty pair pedantic;

One adultrous, as hungry he ; with equal
    Parts in women, a lusty corporation.
    O rare sympathies ! happy rakes united !   10

LVIII.

THAT bright Lesbia, Caelius, the self-same
Peerless Lesbia, she than whom Catullus
Self nor family more devoutly cherish'd,
By foul roads, or in every shameful alley,
Strains the vigorous issue of the people.   5

LIX.

POOR Rufa from Bononia Rufulus gallants,
Menenius' errant lady, she that in grave-yards
(You've seen her often) snaps from every pile her meal,
When hotly chasing dusty loaves the fire rolls down,
She felt some half-shorn corpseman and his hand's big
     blow.   . 5

LX.

HADST thou a Libyan lioness on heights all stone,
A Scylla, barking wolvish at the loins' last verge,
To bear thee, O black-hearted, O to shame forsworn,
That unto supplication in my last sad need
Thou mightst not harken, deaf to ruth, a beast, no
     man?   5

LXI.

GOD, on verdurous Helicon
     Dweller, child of Urania,
     Thou that draw'st to the man the fair
Maiden, O Hymenaeus, O
     Hymen, O Hymenaeus: 5

Wreathe thy brows in amaracus'
     Fragrant blossom; an aureat
     Veil be round thee; approach, in all
Joy, approach with a luminous
     Foot, a sandal of amber.   10

Come, for jolly the time, awake.
     Chant in melody musical
     Hymns of bridal; on earth a foot
Beating, hands to the winds above
     Torches oozily swinging.   15

Such, as she that on Idaly
    Venus dwelleth, appear'd before
    Him, the Phrygian arbiter,
So with Mallius happily
    Happy Junia weddeth.   20

Like some myrtle of Asia
    Bright in airily blossoming
    Boughs, the wood Hamadryades
Nurse with showery dew, to be
    Theirs, a tender plaything.   25

So come to us in haste ; away,
    Leave thy Thespian hollow-arch'd
    Rock, muse-haunted, Aonian,
Drench'd in spray from aloft, the cold
    Drift of Nymph Aganippe.   30

Homeward summon a sovereign
    Wife most passionate, holden in
    Love fast prisoner ; ivy not
Closer closes an elm around,
    Interchangeably trailing.   35

You too with him, O you for whom
    Comes as joyous a time, your own.
    Virgins stainless of heart, arise.
Chant in unison, Hymen, O
    Hymen, O Hymenaeus.   40

That, more readily listening,
    Whiles your song to familiar
    Duty calls him, he hie apace,
Lord of fair paramours, of youth's
    Fair affection uniter.   45

WHO more worthy than he to list
  Lovers wearily languishing ?
  Bends from heaven a sovereign
God adorabler?   Hymen, O
  Hymen, O Hymenaeus.   50

You the father in years for his
  Child beseecheth ; a virginal
  Zone falls slackly to earth for you,
You half-fear in his hankering
  · Lists the groomsman approaching.   55

You from motherly lap the bright
  Girl can sever ; your hand divine
  Gives dominion, ushering
Warm the lover.   O Hymen, O
  Hymen, O Hymenaeus.   60

Nought delightful, if you be far,
  Nought unharmed of envious
  Tongues, Love wins him : if you be near
Much he wins him.   O excellent
  God, that hath not a rival.   65

Houses cannot, if you be far,
  Yield their children, a babe renew
  Sire or mother : if you be near,
Comes renewal.   O excellent
  God, that hath not a rival.   70

If your great ceremonial
  Fail, no champíon yeomanry
  Guards the border.   If you be near
Arms the border.   O excellent
  God, that hath not a rival.   75

FLING the portal apart.   The bride
   Waits.   O see ye the luminous
   Torch-flakes ruddily flickering ?

. . . .
. . . .   80

. . . .
. . . .
. . . .

Nought she hears us : her innocent   (80)
   Eyes do weep to be going.   85

Weep not, lady ; for envious
   Tongue no lovelier owneth, Au-
   Runculeia ; nor any more
Fair saw rosily bright the dawn   (85)
   Leave his chamber in Ocean.   90

Such in many a flowering
   Garden, trimm'd for a lord's delight,
   Stands some delicate hyacinth.
Yet you tarry.   The day declines.   (90)
   Forth, fair bride, to the people.   95

Forth, fair bride, to the people, if
   So it likes you, a-listening
   Words that please us.   O eye ye yon
Torches ruddily flickering?   (95)
   Forth, fair bride, to the people.   100

Husband never of yours shall haunt
   Stained wanton, a mutinous
   Fancy shamefully following,
Tire not ever, or e'er from your   (100)
   Dainty bosom unyoke him.   105

He more lithe than a vine amid
    Trees, that, mazily folded, it
    Clasps and closes, in amorous
Arms shall close thee. The day declines. (105)
    Forth, fair bride, to the people. 110

Couch of pleasure, *O odorous*
    Couch, whose gorgeous apparellings,
    Silver-purple, on Indian
Woods do rest them ; adown the bright
    Feet in ivory glisten ; · 115

When thy lord in his hour attains,
    What large extasy, while the night (110)
    Fleets, or noon the meridian
Passes thoro'. The day declines.
    Forth, fair bride, to the people. 120

·

LIFT the torches aloft in air,
    Boys : the fiery veil is here. (115)
    Come, to measure your hymn rehearse.
Hymen, O Hymenaeus, O
    Hymen, O Hymenaeus. 125

Nor withhold ye the countryman's
    Ribald raillery Fescenine. (120)
    Nor if happily boys declare
Thy dominion attaint, refuse,
    Youth, the nuts to be flinging. 130

Fling, O womanish youth ; the boys
    Ask thee charity. Time agone (125)
    Toys and folly ; to-day begins
Our high duty, Talassius.
    Hasten, youth, to be flinging. 135

Thou didst surely but yestereve
   Mock the women, a favourite   (130)
   Far above them : anon the first
Beard, the razor. Alack, alas !
   Hasten, youth, to be flinging.   140

You, whom odorous oils declare
   Bridegroom, swerve not ; a slippery (135)
   Love calls lightly, but yet refrain.
Hymen, O Hymenaeus, O
   Hymen, O Hymenaeus.   145

Lawful only did e'er delight
   You, we know ; but it is not, O   (140)
   Husband, lawful as heretofore.
Hymen, O Hymenaeus, O
   Hymen, O Hymenaeus.   150

Bride, thou also, if he demand
   Aught, refuse not, assent, obey.   (145)
   Love can angrily pipe adieu.
Hymen, O Hymenaeus, O
   Hymen, O Hymenaeus.   155

Look ! thy mansion, a sovereign
   Home most goodly, by him to thee (150)
   Given. Reign as a queen within,
Hymen, O Hymenaeus, O
   Hymen, O Hymenaeus.   160

Still when hoary decrepitude,
   Shaking wintery brows benign,   (155)
   Nods a tremulous Yes to all.
Hymen, O Hymenaeus, O
   Hymen, O Hymenaeus.   165

WITH fair augury smite the blest
   Threshold, sunnily glistening   (160)
   Feet : yon ivory door approach,
Hymen, O Hymenaeus, O
   Hymen, O Hymenaeus.   170

See one seated, a banqueter.
   'Tis thy lord on a Tyrian   (165)
   Couch : his spirit is all to thee.
Hymen, O Hymenaeus, O
   Hymen, O Hymenaeus.   175

Not less surely in him than in ..
   Thee love lighteth a bosoming   (170)
   Flame ; but deeper, a fire within.
Hymen, O Hymenaeus, O
   Hymen, O Hymenaeus.   180

.   .   .   .
  .   .   .   .
  .   .   .   .
.   .   .   .
    185

Thou, whose purple her arm, the slim
   Arm, props happily, boy, depart.   (175)
   Time the bride be at entering.
Hymen, O Hymenaeus, O
   Hymen, O Hymenaeus.   190

You in chastity tried the long
   Years, good women of agedest   (180)
   Husbands, lay ye the bride to-night.
Hymen, O Hymenaeus, O
   Hymen, O Hymenaeus.   195

HUSBAND, stay not : a bride within
    Coucheth ready, the flowering   (185)
    Spring less lovely ; a countenance
White as parthenice, beyond
    Yellow poppy to gaze on.   200

Thou, so help me the favouring
    Gods immortal, as heavenly   (190)
    Fair art also, adorned of
Venus' bounty.   The day declines.
    Come nor tarry to greet her.   205

Not too slothfully tarrying,
    Thou art here.   Benediction of   (195)
    Venus help thee, a man without
Shame of blameless, a love that is
    Honest frankly revealing.   210

Dust of infinite Africa,
    Stars that sparkle, a myriad   (200)
    Host, who measureth, your delights
He shall tell them, ineffable,
    Multitudinous, over.   215

Make your happy delight, renew'd
    Soon in children.   A glorious   (205)
    Name and olden is ill without
Children, unto the first a new
    Stock as goodly begetting.   220

Some Torquatus, a beauteous
    Babe, on motherly breasts to thee   (210)
    Stretching, father, his innocent
Hands, smile softly from inchoate
    Lips half-open a welcome.   225

Like his father, a Mallius
   New presented, of every   (215)
   Eyeing stranger allowed his own ;
Mother's chastity moulded in
   Features childly revealing.   230

Glory speak of him issuing
   Child of mother as excellent   (220)
   She, as only that age-renown'd
Wife, whose story Telemachus
   Blazons, Penelopea.   235

Virgins, close ye the door.   Enough
   This our carol.   O happiest   (225)
   Lovers, jollity live with you.
Still that genial youth to love's
   Consummation attend ye.   240

LXII.

YOUTHS.

HESPER is here ; rise youths, rise all of you ; high on
   Olympus
Hesper his orb long-look'd for aloft 'gins slowly to kindle.
Time is now to arise, from tables costly to part us ;
Now doth a virgin approach, now soundeth a glad
   Hymenaeal.

Hymen O Hymenaeus, O Hymen come Hymenaeus.   5

VIRGINS.

See ye yon youthful band ? O, maidens, rise ye to meet
   them.
Comes not Night's bright bearer a fire o'er Oeta re-
   vealing ?
Surely ; for even now, in a moment all have arisen,

Not for nought have arisen ; a song waits, goodly to
    gaze on.

Hymen O Hymenaeus, O Hymen come Hymenaeus.   10

YOUTHS.

No light victory this, O comrades, ready before us.
    Busy the virgins muse, their practis'd ditty recalling,
    Muse nor shall miscarry ; a song for memory waits us.
    Rightly ; for all their souls do inwards labour in issue.

We—our thoughts one way, our ears have drifted another, 15
    So comes worthy defeat ; no victory calls to the careless.
    Come then, in even race let thought their melody rival ;
    They must open anon ; 'twere better anon be replying.

Hymen O Hymenaeus, O Hymen come Hymenaeus.

VIRGINS.

Hesper, moveth in heaven a light more tyrannous ever? 20
    Thou from a mother's arms canst wrest her daughter
        asunder,   [ing,
    Wrest from a mother's arms her daughter woefully cling-
    Then to the burning youth his virgin beauty deliver.
    Foes in a new-sack'd town, when wrought they crueller
        ever ?

Hymen O Hymenaeus, O Hymen come Hymenaeus.   25

YOUTHS.

Hesper, shineth in heaven a light more genial ever ?
    Thou with a bridal flame true lovers' unity crownest,
    All which duly the men, which plighted duly the parents,
    Then completed alone, when thou in splendour awakest.
    When shone an happier hour than thy god-speeded
        arriving ?   30

Hymen O Hymenaeus, O Hymen come Hymenaeus.

VIRGINS.

Sisters, Hesper a fellow of our bright company taketh.

. . . .
. . . .
. . . . 35
. . . .
. . . .
. . . .

Hymen O Hymenaeus, O Hymen come Hymenaeus.

YOUTHS.

. . . . 40
. . . .

Hesper, awaiting thee each sentinel holdeth alarum.
Night veils love's false thieves; thieves still when,
    Hesper, another
Name, but unalter'd still, thou tak'st them surely,
    returning. (35)
Yet be the maidens pleas'd in woeful fancy to chide
    thee. 45
Maybe for all they chide, their hearts do inly desire thee.

Hymen O Hymenaeus, O Hymen come Hymenaeus.

VIRGINS.

Look in a garden-croft when a flower privily growing,
    Hid from grazing kine, by ploughshare never
    y-broken, (40)
    Strok'd by the breeze, by the sun nurs'd sturdily, rear'd
    by the showers ; 50
Many a wistful boy, and maidens many desire it :

Yet if a slender nail hath nipt his bloom to deflour it,
    Never a wistful boy, nor maidens any desire it :

Such is a girl untoy'd with as yet, yet lovely to kinsmen ; (45)

Once her body profan'd, her flow'r of chastity blighted, 55
Boys no more she delights, nor seems so lovely to
    maidens ;

Hymen O Hymenaeus, O Hymen come Hymenaeus.

YOUTHS.

Look as a lone lorn vine in a bare field sorrily growing,
    Never an arm uplifts, no grape to maturity ripens, (50)

Only with headlong weight her tender body declining, 60
    Bows, till topmost spray and roots meet feebly together ;
    Her no peasant swain, nor bullock tendeth her ever :

Yet to the bachelor elm if marriage-fortune unite her,
    Many a peasant tills and bullocks many about her; (55)

Such is a maid untoy'd with as yet, in loneliness aging; 65
    Wins she a bridegroom meet, in time's warm fulness
        arriving,
    So to the man more dear, and less unlovely to parents.

O then, clasp thy love, nor fight, fair maiden, against him.
    Sin 'twere surely to fight ; thy father gave to his arms
        thee,   (60)
    Father's self and mother ; obey nor wrongly defy them. 70
    . . . .

Virgin's crown thou claim'st not alone, but partly the
        parents,
    Father's one whole part, one goes to the mother allotted,
    Rests one only to thee ; O fight not with them alone
        thou,
    Both to a son their rights and both their dowry
        deliver.   ·   75 (65)

Hymen O Hymenaeus, O Hymen come Hymenaeus.

LXIII.

IN a swift ship Attis hasting over ocean a mariner
 When he gained the wood, the Phrygian, with a foot of
  agility,
 When he near'd the leafy forest, dark sanctuary divine ;
 By unearthly fury frenzied, a bewildered agony,   ʼ
 With a flint of edge he shatter'd to the ground his
  humanity.   5
 Then aghast to see the lost limbs, the deform'd inutility,
 While still the gory dabble did anew the soil pollute,
 With a snowy palm the woman took affrayed a taborine. ˙
 Taborine, the trump that hails thee, Cybele, thy initiant.
 Then a dainty finger heaving to the tremulous hide o'
  the bull,   10
 He began this invocation to the company, spirit-awed.

" To the groves, ye sexless eunuchs, in assembly to
  Cybele,
 Lost sheep that err rebellious to the lady Dindymene ;
 Ye, who all awing for exile in a country of aliens,
 My unearthly rule obeying to be with me, my retinue, 15
 Could aby the surly salt seas' mid inexorability,
 Could in utter hate to lewdness your sex dishabilitate ;

Let a gong clash glad emotion, set a giddy fury to roam,
All slow delay be banish'd, thither hie ye thither away
To the Phrygian home, the wild wood, to the sanctuary
  divine ;   20

 Where rings the noisy cymbal, taborines are in echoing,
 On a curvèd oat the Phrygian deep pipeth a melody,

E

With a fury toss the Maenads clad in ivies a frolic head,
To a barbarous ululation the religious orgy wakes,
Where fleets across the silence Cybele's holy family ; 25
Thither hie we, so beseems us; to a mazy measure
    away."

Thus as Attis, a woman, Attis, not a woman, urg'd the
    rest,
On a sudden yell'd in huddling agitation every tongue,
Taborines give airy murmur, give a clangorous echo
    gongs,
With a rush the brotherhood hastens to the woods,
    the bosom of Ide. 30
Then in agony, breathless, errant, flush'd wearily,
    cometh on
Taborine behind him, Attis, thoro' leafy glooms a guide,
As a restive heifer yields not to the cumbrous onerous
    yoke.
Thither hie the votaress eunuchs with an emulous
    alacrity.
Now faintly sickly plodding to the goddess's holy
    shrine, 35
They took the rest which easeth long toil, nor ate
    withal.
Slow sleep descends on eyelids ready drowsily to
    decline,
In a soft repose departeth the devout spirit-agony.
When awoke the sun, the golden, that his eyes heaven-
    orient
Scann'd lustrous air, the rude seas, earth's massy
    solidity, 40
When he smote the shadowy twilight with his healthy
    team sublime,
Then arous'd was Attis; o'er him sleep hastily fled away

To Pasithea's arms immortal with a tremulous hovering.
But awaked from his reposing, the delirious anguish
o'er,
When as Attis' heart recalled him to the past
solitarily, 45
Saw clearly where he stood, what, an annihilate apathy,
With a soul that heaved within him, to the water he
fled again.
Then as o'er the waste of ocean with a rainy eye he gazed
To the land of home he murmur'd miserable a soliloquy.

" MOTHER-HOME of all affection, dear home, my nativity, 50
Whom in anguish I deserting, as in hatred a runaway
From a master, hither have hurried to the lonely woods
of Ide,

To be with the snows, the wild beasts, in a wintery domicile,
To be near each savage houser that a surly fury
provokes,
What horizon, O beloved, may attain to thee
anywhere ? 55

Yet an eyeless orb is yearning ineffectually to thee.
For a little ere returneth the delirious hour again.

Shall a homeless Attis hie him to the groves unin-
habited ?
Shall he leave a country, wealth, friends? bid a sire, a
mother, adieu?
The palaestra lost, the forum, the gymnasium, the
course ? 60

O unhappy, fall a-weeping, thou unhappy soul, for aye.

For is honour of any semblance, any beauty but of it I ?

Who, a woman here, in order was a man, a youth, a boy,
To the sinewy ring a fam'd flower, the gymnasium's
    applause.

With a throng about the portal, with a populace in the
    gate,   65
    With a flowery coronal hanging upon every column of
        home,
    When anew my chamber open'd, as awoke the sunny
        morn.

O am I to live the god's slave ? feodary be to Cybele ?
Or a Maenad I, an eunuch ? or a part of a body slain ?

Or am I to range the green tracts upon Ida snowy-chill? 70
    Be beneath the stately caverns colonnaded of Asia ?
    Be with hind that haunts the covert, or in hursts that
        house the boar ?

Woe, woe the deed accomplish'd ! woe, woe, the shame
    to me !"

From rosy lips ascending when approached the gusty cry
    To celestial ears recording such a message inly
        borne,   75
    Cybele, the thong relaxing from a lion-haled yoke,
    Said, aleft the goad addressing to the foe that awes the
        flocks—

"COME, a service ; haste, my brave one ; let a fury the
    madman arm,
    Let a fury, a frenzy prick him to return to the wood
        again,
    This is he my hest declineth, the unheedy, the run-
        away.   80

From an angry tail refuse not to abide the sinewy stroke,

To a roar let all the regions echo answer everywhere,
On a nervy neck be tossing that uneasy tawny mane."

So in ire she spake, adjusting disunitedly then her yoke
At his own rebuke the lion doth his heart to a fury
    spur, 85
With a step, a roar, a bursting unarrested of any brake.
But anear the foamy places when he came, to the
    frothy beach,
When he saw the sexless Attis by the seas' level opaline,
Then he rushed upon him ; affrighted to the wintery
    wood he flew,
Cybele's for aye, for all years, in her order a votaress. 90
Holy deity, great Cybele, holy lady Dindymene,
Be to me afar for ever that inordinate agony.
O another hound to madness, O another hurry to rage !

LXIV.

BORN on Pelion height, so legend hoary relateth,
    Pines once floated adrift on Neptune billowy streaming
    On to the Phasis flood, to the borders Æætean.
    Then did a chosen array, rare bloom of valorous Argos,
    Fain from Colchian earth her fleece of glory to ravish, 5
    Dare with a keel of swiftness adown salt seas to be
        fleeting,
    Swept with fir-blades oary the fair level azure of Ocean.
    Then that deity bright, who keeps in cities her high ward,
    Made to delight them a car, to the light breeze airily
        scudding,
    Texture of upright pine with a keel's curved rondure
        uniting. 10
    That first sailer of all burst ever on Amphitrite.

Scarcely the forward snout tore up that wintery water,
  Scarcely the wave foamed white to the reckless harrow
    of oarsmen,
  Straight from amid white eddies arose wild faces of
    Ocean,
  Nereid, earnest-eyed, in wonderous admiration.   15
  Then, not after again, saw ever mortal unharmed
  Sea-born Nymphs unveil limbs flushing naked about
    them,
  Stark to the nursing breasts from foam and billow
    arising.
  Then, so stories avow, burn'd Peleus hotly to Thetis,
  Then to a mortal lover abode not Thetis unheeding, 20
  Then did a father agree Peleus with Thetis unite him.

O in an aureat hour, O born in bounteous ages,
  God-sprung heroes, hail : hail, mother of all bene-
    diction,
  You my song shall address, you melodies everlasting.
  Thee most chiefly, supreme in glory of heavenly
    bridal,   25
  Peleus, stately defence of Thessaly.   Iuppiter even
  Gave thee his own fair love, thy mortal pleasure
    approving.
  Thee could Thetis inarm, most beauteous Ocean-
    daughter ?
  Tethys adopt thee, her own dear grandchild's wooer
    usurping?
  Ocean, who earth's vast globe with a watery girdle
    inorbeth?   30

When the delectable hour those days did fully deter-
    mine,
  Straightway then in crowds all Thessaly flock'd to the
    palace,

Thronging hosts uncounted, a company joyous ap-
    proaching.
Many a gift they carry, delight their faces illumines.
Left is Scyros afar, and Phthia's bowery Tempe,   35
Vacant Crannon's homes, unvisited high Larisa,
Towards Pharsalia's halls, Pharsalia's only they hie
    them.

Bides no tiller afield; necks soften of oxen in idlesse;
    Feel not a prong'd crook'd hoe lush vines all weedily
        trailing;
    Tears no steer deep clods with a downward coulter
        unearthed ; ·   40
    Prunes no hedger's bill broad-verging verdurous arbours;
    Steals a deforming rust on ploughs left rankly to
        moulder.

But that sovran abode, each sumptuous inly retiring
    Chamber, aflame with gold, with silver, is all re-
        splendent ;
    Thrones gleam ivory-white; cup-crown'd blaze brightly
        the tables ;   45
    All the domain with treasure of empery gaudily flushes.

There, set deeply within the remotest centre, a bridal
    Bed doth a goddess inarm ; smooth ivory glossy from
        Indies,
    Robed in roseate hues, rich seashells' purple adorning.

It was a broidery freak'd with tissue of images olden,   50
    One whose curious art did blazon valour of heroes.
    Gazing forth from a beach of Dia the billow-resounding,
    Look'd on a vanish'd fleet, on Theseus quickly de-
        parting,
    Restless in unquell'd passion, a feverous heart, Ariadne.

Scarcely her eyes yet seem their seeming clearly to
 vision.   55
You might guess that arous'd from slumber's drowsy
 betrayal,
Sand-engirded, alone, then first she knew desolation.
He the betrayer—his oars with fugitive hurry the waters
Beat, each promise of old to the winds given idly to
 bear them.

Him from amid shore-weeds doth Minos' daughter, in
 anguish   60
Rigid, a Bacchant-form, dim-gazing stonily follow,
Stonily still, wave-tost on a sea of troublous affliction.
Holds not her yellow locks the tiara's feathery tissue ;
Veils not her hidden breast light brede of drapery
 woven ;
Binds not a cincture smooth her bosom's orbed
 emotion.   65
Widely from each fair limb that footward-fallen apparel
Drifts its lady before, in billowy salt loose-playing.

Not for silky tiara nor amice gustily floating
Recks she at all any more ; thee, Theseus, ever her
 earnest
Heart, all clinging thought, all chained fancy re-
 quireth.   70
Ah unfortunate ! whom with miseries ever crazing,
Thorns in her heart deep planted, affray'd Erycina to
 madness,
From that earlier hour, when fierce for victory Theseus
Started alert from a beach deep-inleted of Piræus,
Gain'd Gortyna's abode, injurious halls of oppression. 75

Once, 'tis sung in stories, a dire distemper atoning
Death of an ill-blest prince, Androgeos, angrily
 slaughter'd,

Taxed of her youthful array, her maidenly bloom fresh-
glowing,
Feast to the monster bull, Cecropia, ransom-laden.
Then, when a plague so deadly, the garrison under-
mining, 80
Spent that slender city, his Athens dearly to rescue,
Sooner life Theseus and precious body did offer,
Ere his country to Crete freight corpses, a life in seem-
ing.
So with a ship fast-fleeted, a gale blown gently behind
him,
Push'd he his onward journey to Minos' haughty
dominion. 85

Him for very delight when a virgin fondly desiring
Gazed on, a royal virgin, in odours silkily nestled,
Pure from a maiden's couch, from a mother's pillowy
bosom,
Like some myrtle, anear Eurotas' water arising,
Like earth's myriad hues, spring's progeny, rais'd to
the breezes ; 90
Droop'd not her eyes their gaze unquenchable, ever-
burning
Save when in each charm'd limb to the depths enfolded,
a sudden
Flame blazed hotly within her, in all her marrow
abiding.

O thou cruel of heart, thou madding worker of anguish,
Boy immortal, of whom joy springs with misery blend-
ing, 95
Yea, thou queen of Golgi, of Idaly leaf-embower'd,
O'er what a fire love-lit, what billows wearily tossing,
Drave ye the maid, for a guest so sunnily lock'd deep
sighing.

What most dismal alarms her swooning fancy did echo!
Oft what a sallower hue than gold's cold glitter upon
  her!   100
Whiles, heart-hungry in arms that monster deadly to
  combat,
Theseus drew towards death or victory, guerdon of
  honour.
Yet not lost the devotion, or offer'd idly the virgin's
Gifts, as her unvoic'd lips breathed incense faintly to
  heaven.

As on Taurus aloft some oak agitatedly waving   105
  Tosses his arms, or a pine cone-mantled, oozily rinded,
  When as his huge gnarled trunk in furious eddies a
    whirlwind
  Riving wresteth amain; down falleth he, upward hoven,
  Falleth on earth; far, near, all crackles brittle around him,
  So to the ground Theseus his fallen foeman abasing, 110
  Slew, that his horned front toss'd vainly, a sport to the
    breezes.
  Thence in safety, a victor, in height of glory returned,
  Guiding errant feet to a thread's impalpable order.
  Lest, upon egress bent thro' tortuous aisles labyrinthine,
  Walls of blindness, a maze unravell'd ever, elude
    him.   115

Yet, for again I come to the former story, beseems not
  Linger on all done there; how left that daughter a
    gazing
  Father, a sister's arms, her mother woefully clinging,
  Mother, who o'er that child moan'd desperate, all heart-
    broken;
  How not in home that maid, in Theseus only de-
    lighted;   120
  How her ship on a shore of foaming Dia did harbour;

How, when her eyes lay bound in slumber's shadowy
  prison,
He forsook, forgot her, a wooer traitorous-hearted:

Oft, say stories, at heart with frenzied fantasy burning,
  Pour'd she, a deep-wrung breast, clear-ringing cries of
    oppression;   125
  Sometimes mournfully clomb to the mountain's rugged
    ascension,
  Straining thence her vision across wide surges of ocean;
  Now to the brine ran forth, upsplashing freshly to meet
    her,
  Lifting raiment fine her thighs which softly did open;
  Last, when sorrow had end, these words thus spake she
    lamenting,   130
  While from a mouth tear-stain'd chill sobs gushed
    dolorous ever.

' LOOK, is it here, false heart, that rapt from country, from
    altar,
  Household altar ashore, I wander, falsely deserted?
  Ah! is it hence, Theseus, that against high heaven a
    traitor
Homeward thou thy vileness, alas thy perjury bearest? 135

Might not a thought, one thought, thy cruel counsel
    abating
  Sway thee tender? at heart rose no compassion or
    any
  Mercy, to bend thy soul, or me for pity deliver?

Yet not this thy promise of old, thy dearly remembered
  Voice, not these the delights thou bad'st thy poor one
    inherit;   140
  Nay, but wedlock happy, but envied joy hymeneal;

All now melted in air, with a light wind emptily fleeting.

LET not a woman trust, since that first treason, a lover's
  Desperate oath, none hope true lover's promise is
    earnest.
  They, while fondly to win their amorous humour
    essayeth,   145
  Fear no covetous oath, all false free promises heed not;
  They if once lewd pleasure attain unruly possession,
Lo they fear not promise, of oath or perjury reck not.

Yet indeed, yet I, when floods of death were around thee,
  Set thee on high, did rather a brother choose to defend
    not,   150
  Ere I, in hate's last hour, false heart, fail'd thee to deliver.
Now, for a goodly reward, to the beasts they give me,
  the flying
  Fowls; no handful of earth shall bury me, pass'd to the
    shadows.

WHAT grim lioness yeaned thee, aneath what rock's deso-
  lation?
  What wild sea did bear, what billows foamy regorged
    thee?   155
  Seething sand, or Scylla the snare, or lonely Charybdis?
If for a life's dear joy comes back such only requital?

Hadst not a will with spousal an honour'd wife to receive
  me?
  Awed thee a father stern, cross age's churlish avising?
  Yet to your household thou, your kindred palaces
    olden,   160
  Might'st have led me, to wait, joy-filled, a retainer upon
    thee,

Now in waters clear thy feet like ivory laving,
Clothing now thy bed with crimson's gorgeous apparel.

Yet to the brutish winds why moan I longer unheeded,
  Crazy with an ill wrong? They senseless, voiceless,
    inhuman   165
  Utter'd cry they hear not, in answers hollow reply not.
  He rides far already, the mid sea's boundary cleaving,
  Strays no mortal along these weeds stretched lonely
    about me.
  Thus to my utmost need chance, spitefuller injury dealing,
Grudges an ear, where yet might lamentation have
    entry.   170

JOVE, almighty, supreme, O would that never in early
  Time on Gnossian earth great Cecrops' navies had
    harbour'd,
  Ne'er to that unquell'd bull with a ransom of horror
    atoning,
  Moor'd on Crete his cable a shipman's wily dishonour.
  Never in youth's fair shape such ruthless stratagem
    hiding   175
He, that vile one, a guest found with us a safe habitation.

Whither flee then afar? what hope, poor lost one, up-
  holds thee?
  Mountains Idomenean? alas, broad surges of ocean
  Part us, a rough rude space of flowing water, asunder.
  Trust in a father's help? how trust, whom darkly
    deserting,   180
  Him I turned to alone, my brother's bloody defier?
  Nay, but a loyal lover, a hand pledg'd surely, shall
    ease me.
Surely; for o'er wide water his oars move flexibly fleeting.

Also a desert lies this region, a tenantless island,
 Nowhere open way, seas splash in circle around me, 185
 Nowhere flight, no glimmer of hope ; all mournfully
     silent,
Loneliness all, all points me to death, death only re-
     maining.

YET these luminous orbs shall sink not feebly to darkness,
 Yet from grief-worn limbs shall feeling wholly depart not,
 Till to the gods I cry, the betrayed, for justice on evil, 190
Sue for life's last mercy the great federation of heaven.

Then, O sworn to requite man's evil wrathfully, Powers
 Gracious, on whose grim brows, with viper tresses
     inorbed,
 Looks red-breathing forth your bosom's feverous anger ;

Now, yea now come surely, to these loud miseries
     harken,   195
 All I cry, the afflicted, of inmost marrow arising,
 Desolate, hot with pain, with blinding fury bewilder'd.

Yet, for of heart they spring, grief's children truly begotten,
 Verily, Gods, these moans you will not idly to perish.
 But with counsel of evil as he forsook me deceiving, 200
Death to his house, to his heart, bring also counsel of evil.

WHEN from an anguish'd heart these words stream'd
     sorrowful upwards,
 Words which on iron deeds did sue for deadly requital,
 Bow'd with a nod of assent almighty the ruler of heaven.
 With that dreadful motion aneath earth's hollow, the
     ruffled   205
 Ocean shook, and stormy the stars 'gan tremble in ether.

Thereto his heart thick-sown with blindness cloudily
    dark'ning,
Thought not of all those words, Theseus, from memory
    fallen,
Words which his heedful soul had kept immovable ever.
Nor to his eager sire fair token of happy returning 210
Rais'd, when his eyes safe-sighted Erectheus' populous
    haven.
Once, so stories tell, when Pallas' city behind him
Leaving, Theseus' fleet to the winds given hopefully
    parted,
Clasping then his son spake Aegeus, straitly com-
    manding.

SON, mine only delight, than life more lovely to gaze
    on,   215
   Son, whom needs it faints me to launch full-tided on
      hazards,
   Whom my winter of years hath laid so lately before me :

Since my fate unkindly, thy own fierce valour unheeding,
   Needs must wrest thee away, ere yet these dimly-lit
      eye-balls
   Feed to the full on thee, thy worshipt body behold-
      ing ;   220

Neither in exultation of heart I send thee a-warring ;
   Nor to the fight shalt bear fair fortune's happier earnest ;
Rather, first in cries mine heart shall lighten her anguish,
   When grey locks I sully with earth, with sprinkle of ashes ;

Next to the swaying mast shall a sail hang duskily
    swinging ;   225
So this grief, mine own, this burning sorrow within me,
Want not a sign, dark shrouds of Iberia, sombre as iron.

Then, if haply the queen, lone ranger on haunted Itonus,
 Pleas'd to defend our people, Erectheus' safe habitations,
 Frown not, allow thine hand that bull all redly to
  slaughter,   230

Look that warily then deep-laid in steady remembrance,
 These our words grow greenly, nor age move on to
  deface them ;

Soon as on home's fair hills thine eyes shall signal a
  welcome,
 See that on each straight yard down droop their
  funeral housings,
 Whitely the tight-strung cordage a sparkling canvas
  aloft swing,   235

Which to behold straightway with joy shall cheer me,
  with inward
 Joy, when a prosperous hour shall bring to thee happy
  returning.

So for a while that charge did Theseus faithfully cherish.
 Last, it melted away, as a cloud which riven in ether
 Breaks to the blast, high peak and spire snow-silvery
  leaving.   240
 But from a rock's wall'd eyrie the father wistfully gazing,
 Father whose eyes, care-dimm'd, wore hourly for ever a-
  weeping,
 Scarcely the wind-puff'd sail from afar 'gan darken
  upon him,
 Down the precipitous heights headlong his body he
  hurried,
 Deeming Theseus surely by hateful destiny taken.   245
 So to a dim death-palace, alert from victory, Theseus
 Came, what bitter sorrow to Minos' daughter his evil
 Perjury gave, himself with an even sorrow atoning.

She, as his onward keel still moved, still mournfully
    follow'd ;
Passion-stricken, her heart a tumultuous image of
    ocean. 250

Also upon that couch, flush'd youthfully, breathless Iacchus
    Roam'd with a Satyr-band, with Nisa-begot Sileni ;
    Seeking thee, Ariadna, aflame thy beauty to ravish.
    Wildly behind they rushed and wildly before to the folly,
    Euhoe rav'd, Euhoe with fanatic heads gyrated ; 255
    Some in womanish hands shook rods cone-wreathed
        above them,
    Some from a mangled steer toss'd flesh yet gorily
        streaming ;
    Some girt round them in orbs, snakes gordian, inter-
        twining ;
    Some with caskets deep did blazon mystical emblems,
    Emblems muffled darkly, nor heard of spirit unholy. 260
    Part with a slender palm taborines beat merrily
        jangling ;
    Now with a cymbal slim would a sharp shrill tinkle
        awaken ;
    Often a trumpeter horn blew murmurous, hoarsely
        resounding.
    Rose on pipes barbaric a jarring music of horror.

Such, wrought rarely, the shapes this quilt did richly
    apparel, 265
    Where to the couch close-clasped it hung thick veils of
        adorning.
    So to the full heart-sated of all their curious eying,
    Thessaly's youth gave place to the Gods high-throned
        in heaven.
    As, when dawn is awake, light Zephyrus even-breathing

F

Brushes a sleeping sea, which slant-wise curved in
    edges   270
Breaks, while mounts Aurora the sun's high journey to
    welcome ;
They, first smitten faintly by his most airy caressing,
Move slow on, light surges a plashing silvery laughter ;
Soon with a waxing wind they crowd them apace, thick-
    fleeting,
Swim in a rose-red glow and far off sparkle in
    Ocean ;   275
So thro' column'd porch and chambers sumptuous
    hieing,
Thither or hither away, that company stream'd, home-
    wending.

First from Pelion height, when they were duly departed,
    Chiron came, in his hand green gifts of flowery forest.
    All that on earth's leas blooms, what blossoms Thessaly
        nursing   280
    Breeds on mountainous heights, what near each
        showery river
    Swells to the warm west-wind, in gales of foison alight-
        ing ;
    These did his own hands bear in girlonds twined of
        all hues,
    That to the perfume sweet for joy laugh'd gaily the
        palace.
    Follow'd straight Penios, awhile his bowery Tempe, 285
    Tempe, shrined around in shadowy woods o'erhanging,
    Left to the bare-limb'd maids Magnesian, airily
        ranging.
    No scant carrier he ; tall root-torn beeches his heavy
    Burden, bays stemm'd stately, in heights exalted
        ascending.

Thereto the nodding plane, and that lithe sister of
youthful 290
Phaethon flame-enwrapt, and cypress in air upspringing:
These in breadths inwoven he heap'd close-twin'd to the
palace,
Whereto the porch wox green, with soft leaves
canopied over.

Him did follow anear, deep heart and wily, Prometheus,
Scarr'd and wearing yet dim traces of early dis-
honour, 295
All which of old his body to flint fast-welded in iron,
Bore and dearly abied, on slippery crags suspended.
Last with his awful spouse, with children goodly, the
sovran
Father approach'd; thou, Phoebus, alone, his warder in
heaven,
Left, with that dear sister, on Idrus ranger eternal. 300
Peleus sister alike and brother in high misprision
Held, nor lifted a torch when Thetis wedded at even.
So when on ivory thrones they rested, snowily
gleaming,
Many a feast high-pil'd did load each table about
them ;
Whiles to a tremor of age their gray infirmity
rocking, 305
Busy began that chant which speaketh surely the
Parcae.

Round them a folding robe their weak limbs aguish
hiding,
Fell bright-white to the feet, with a purple border of
issue.
Wreaths sat on each hoar crown, whose snows flush'd
rosy beneath them ;

F 2

Still each hand fulfilled its pious labour eternal.　310
Singly the left upbore in wool soft-hooded a distaff,
Whereto the right large threads down drawing deftly,
　　with upturn'd
Fingers shap'd them anew ; then thumbs earth-pointed
　　in even
Balance twisted a spindle on orb'd wheels smoothly
　　rotating.
So clear'd softly between and tooth-nipt even it ever 315
Onward moved ; still clung on wan lips, sodden as
　　ashes,
Shreds all woolly from out that soft smooth surface
　　arisen.
Lastly before their feet lay fells, white, fleecy, refulgent,
Warily guarded they in baskets woven of osier.
They, as on each light tuft their voice smote louder
　　approaching,　　　　　·　　　　·　　　　320
Pour'd grave inspiration, a prophet chant to the future,
Chant which an after-time shall tax of vanity never.

O IN valorous acts thy wondrous glory renewing,
　　Rich Aemathia's arm, great sire of a goodlier issue,
　　Hark on a joyous day what prophet-story the sisters 325
　　Open surely to thee ; and you, what followeth after,
Guide to a long-drawn thread and run with destiny,
　　spindles.

Soon shall approach, and bear the delight long-wish'd for
　　of husbands,
　　Hesper, a bride shall approach in starlight happy
　　　presented,
　　Softly to sway thy soul in love's completion abiding, 330
　　Soon in a trance with thee of slumber dreamy to
　　　mingle,

Making smooth round arms thy clasp'd throat sinewy
    pillow.
Trail ye a long-drawn thread and run with destiny,
    spindle ;.

Never hath house closed yet o'er loves so blissful uniting,
    Never love so well his children in harmony knitten, 335
    So as Thetis agrees, as Peleus bendeth according.
Trail ye a long-drawn thread and run with destiny,
    spindles.

You shall a son see born that knows not terror, Achilles,
    One whose back no foe, whose front each knoweth in
        onset ;
    Often a conqueror, he, where feet course swiftly
        together, 340
    Steps of a fire-fleet doe shall leave in his hurry behind
        him.
Trail ye a long-drawn thread and run with destiny,
    spindles.

Him to resist in war, no champion hero ariseth,
    Then on Phrygian earth when carnage Trojan is
        utter'd ;
    Then when a long sad strife shall Troy's crown'd city
        beleaguer, 345
    Waste her a third false heir from Pelops wary descend-
        ing.
Trail ye a long-drawn thread and run with destiny,
    spindles.

His unmatchable acts, his deeds of glorious honour,
    Oft shall mothers speak o'er sons untimely departed ;
    While from crowns earth-bow'd fall loosen'd silvery
        tresses, 350

Beat on shrivell'd breasts weak palms their dusky
defacing.
Trail ye a long-drawn thread and run with destiny,
spindles.

As some labourer ears close-cluster'd lustily lopping,
Under a flaming sun, mows fields ripe-yellow in harvest,
*So, in fury of heart, shall death's stern reaper,
Achilles,*
Charge Troy's children afield and fell them grimly with
iron.   355
Trail ye a long-drawn thread and run with destiny,
spindles.

Deeds of such high glory Scamander's river avoucheth,
Hurried in eddies afar thro' boisterous Hellespontus;
Then when a slaughter'd heap his pathway watery chok-
ing,
Brimmeth a warm red tide and blood with water
allieth.   360
Trail ye a long-drawn thread and run with destiny,
spindles.

Voucher of him last riseth a prey untimely devoted
E'en to the tomb, which mounded in heaps, high, spheri-
cal, earthen,
Grants to the snow-white limbs, to the stricken maiden a
welcome.
Trail ye a long-drawn thread and run with destiny,
spindles.   365

Scarcely the war-worn Greeks shall win such favour of
heaven,
Neptune's bonds of stone from Dardan city to loosen,
. Dankly that high-heav'd grave shall gory Polyxena
crimson.

She as a lamb falls smitten a twin-edg'd falchion under,
Boweth on earth weak knees, her limbs down flingeth
    unheeding. 370
Trail ye a long-drawn thread and run with destiny
    spindles.

Up then, fair paramours, in fond love happily mingle.
  Now in blessed treaty the bridegroom welcome a god-
    dess;
  Now give a bride long-veil'd to her husband's pas-
    sionate yearning.
Trail ye a long-drawn thread and run with destiny,
    spindles. 375

Her when duly the nurse with day-light early revisits,
  Necklace of yester-night—she shall not clasp it about her.
  Trail ye a long-drawn thread and run with destiny,
    spindles.

Nor shall a mother fond, o'er brawls unlovely dis-
    hearten'd,
  Lay her alone, or cease the delight of children await-
    ing. 380
  Trail ye a long-drawn thread and run with destiny
    spindles.

In such prelude old, such good-night ditty to Peleus,
  Sang their deep divination, ineffable, holy, the Parcae.
  Such as in ages past, upon houses godly descending,
  Houses of heroes came, in mortal company present, 385
  Gods high-throned in heaven, while yet was worship in
    honour. ·

Often a sovran Jove, in his own bright temple appearing,
  Yearly, whene'er his day did rites ceremonial usher,

Gazed on an hundred slain, on strong bulls heavily
    falling.
Often on high Parnassus a roving Liber in hurried 390
Frenzy the Thyiads drave, their locks blown loosely,
    before him.
While all Delphi's city in eager jealousy trooping,
Blithely receiv'd their god on fuming festival altars.
Mavors often amidst encounter mortal of armies,
Streaming Triton's queen, or maid Ramnusian awful, 395
Stood in body before them, a fainting host to deliver.

Only when heinous sin earth's wholesome purity blasted,
    When from covetous hearts fled justice sadly retreating,
    Then did a brother his hands dye deep in blood of a
        brother,
    Lightly the son forgat his parents' piteous ashes.   400
    Lightly the son's young grave his father pray'd for, an
        unwed
    Maiden, a step-dame fair in freer luxury clasping.
    Then did mother unholy to son that knew not abase her,
    Shamefully, fear'd not unholy the blessed dead to dis-
        honour.
    Human, inhuman alike, in wayward infamy blend-
        ing,   405
    Turned far from us away that righteous counsel of
        heaven.
    Therefore proudly the Gods such sinful company view
        not,
    Bear not day-light clear upon immortality breathing.

LXV.

THOUGH, outworn with sorrow, with hours of torturous
    anguish,
    Ortalus, I no more tarry the Muses among ;
Though from a fancy deprest fair blooms of poesy budding
    Rise not at all ; such grief rocks me, uneasily stirr'd :

Coldly but even now mine own dear brother in ebbing   5
    Lethe his ice-wan feet laveth, a shadowy ghost.
He whom Troy's deep bosom, a shore Rhoetean above
    him,
    Rudely denies these eyes, heavily crushes in earth.

Ah ! no more to address thee, or hear thy kindly replying,
    Brother ! O e'en than life round me delightfuller yet, 10
Ne'er to behold thee again ! Still love shall fail not
    alone in
    Fancy to muse death's dark elegy, closely to weep.
Closely as under boughs of dimmest shadow the pensive
    Daulian ever moans Itys in agony slain.

Yet mid such desolation a verse I tender of ancient   15
    Battiades, new-drest, Ortalus, wholly for you.
Lest to the roving winds these words all idly deliver'd,
    Seem too soon from a frail memory fallen away.

E'en as a furtive gift, sent, some love-apple, a-wooing,
    Leaps from breast of a coy maiden, a canopy pure ; 20
There forgotten alas, mid vestments silky reposing,—
    Soon as a mother's step starts her, it hurleth adown :
Straight to the ground, dash'd forth ungently, the gift
    shoots headlong ;
    She in tell-tale cheeks glows a disorderly shame.

LXVI.

HE whose glance scann'd clearly the lights uncounted of
    ether,
  Found when arises a star, sinks in his haven again,
How yon eclipsed sun glares luminous obscuration,
  How in seasons due vanishes orb upon orb ;
How 'neath Latmian heights fair Trivia stealthily
    banish'd   5
  Falls, from her upward path lured by a lover awhile ;
That same sage, that Conon, a lock of great Berenice
  Saw me, in heavenly-bright deification afar
Lustrous, a gleaming glory ; to gods full many devoted,
  Whiles she her arms in prayer lifted, as ivory
    smooth ;   10
In that glorious hour when, flush'd with a new hymeneal,
  Hotly the King to deface outer Assyria sped,
Bearing ensigns sweet of that soft struggle a night brings,
  When from a virgin's arms spoils he had happily won.

Stands it an edict true that brides hate Venus? or ever 15
  Falsely the parents' joy dashes a showery tear,
When to the nuptial door they come in rainy beteem-
    ing ?
  Now to the Gods I swear, tears be hypocrisy then.
So mine own queen taught me in all her weary lament-
    ings,
  Whiles her bridegroom bold set to the battle a
    face.   20
What ? for an husband lost thou weptst not gloomily
    lying ?
  Rather a brother dear, forced for a while to depart ?
This, when love's sharp grief was gnawing inly to waste
    thee !

Ah poor wife ! whose soul steep'd in unhappiness all,
    Fell from reason away, nor abode thy senses ! A nobler   25
    Spirit had I erewhile known thee, a fiery child.

Pass'd that deed forgotten, a royal wooer had earn'd thee ?
    Deed that braver none ventureth ever again ?
Yet what sorrow to lose thy lord, what murmur of anguish !
    Jove, how rain'd those tears brush'd from a passionate eye !   30
Who is this could wean thee, a God so mighty, to falter?
    May not a lover live from the beloved afar?
Then for a spouse so goodly, before each spirit of heaven,
    Me thou vowd'st, with slain oxen, a vast hecatomb,
Home if again he alighted. Awhile and Asia crouching   35
    Humbly to Egypt's realm added a boundary new ;
I, in starry return to the ranks dedicated of heaven,
    Debt of an ancient vow sum in a bounty to-day.

Full of sorrow was I, fair queen, thy brows to abandon,
    Full of sorrow ; in oath answer, adorable head.   40
Evil on him that oath who sweareth falsely soever !
    Yet in a strife with steel who can a victory claim?
Steel could a mountain abase, no loftier any thro' heaven's
    Cupola Thia's child lifteth his axle above,
Then, when a new-born sea rose Mede-uplifted ; in Athos'   45
    Centre his ocean-fleet floated a barbarous host.

What shall a weak tress do, when powers so mighty re-
    sist not?
Jove! may Chalybes all perish, a people accurst,
Perish who earth's hid veins first labour'd dimly to
    quarry,
    Clench'd in a molten mass iron, a ruffian heart!   50

Scarcely the sister-locks were parted dolefully weeping,
    Straight that brother of young Memnon, in Africa
    born,
Came, and shook thro' heaven his pennons oary, before
    me,
    Winged, a queen's proud steed, Locrian Arsinoë.
So flew with me aloft thro' darkening shadow of
    heaven,   55
    There to a god's pure breast laid me, to Venus's arms.
Him Zephyritis' self had sent to the task, her servant,
    She from realms of Greece borne to Canopus of yore.
There, that at heav'n's high porch, not one sole crown,
    Ariadne's,
    Golden above those brows `Ismaros' youth did
    adore,   60
Starry should hang, set alone; but luminous I might
    glisten,
    Vow'd to the Gods, bright spoil won from an aureat
    head;
While to the skies I clomb still ocean-dewy, the Goddess
    Placed me amid star-spheres primal, a glory to be.

Close to the Virgin bright, to the Lion sulkily gleaming, 65
    Nigh Callisto, a cold child Lycaonian, I
Wheel obliquely to set, and guide yon tardy Bootes
    Where scarce late his car dewy descends to the sea.
Yet tho' nightly the Gods' immortal steps be above me,

Tho' to the white waves dawn gives me, to Tethys,
    again; 70
(Maid of Ramnus, a grace ,I here implore thee, if any
    Word should offend ; so much cannot a terror alarm,
I should veil aught true; not tho' with clamorous uproar
    Rend me the stars; I speak verities hidden at heart):
Lightly for all I reck, so more I sorrow to part me 75
    Sadly from her I serve, part me forever away.
With her, a virgin as yet, I quaff'd no sumptuous
    essence ;
    With her, a bride, I drain'd many a prodigal oiL

Now, O you whom gladly the marriage cresset uniteth,
    See to the bridegroom fond yield ye not amorous
      arms, 80
Throw not back your robes, nor bare your bosom as-
    senting,
    Save from an onyx stream sweetness, a bounty to me.
Yours, in a loyal bed which seek love's privilege, only;
    Yieldeth her any to bear loathed adultery's yoke,
Vile her gifts, and lightly the dust shall drink them un-
    heeding. 85
    Not of vile I seek gifts, nor of infamous, I.
Rather, O unstain'd brides, may concord tarry for ever
    With ye at home, may love with ye for ever abide.
Thou, fair queen, to the stars if looking haply, to Venus
    Lights thou kindle on eves festal of high sacrifice, 90
Leave me the lock, thine own, nor blood nor bounty
    requiring.
    Rather a largesse fair pay to me, envy me not.
Stars dash blindly in one ! so might I glitter a royal
    Tress, let Orion glow next to Aquarius' urn.

LXVII.

CATULLUS.

O TO the goodman fair, O welcome alike to the father,
    Hail, and Jove's kind grace shower his help upon
    you !
Door, that of old, men say, wrought Balbus ready
    obeisance,
    Once, when his home, time was, lodged him, a master
    in years;
Door, that again, men say, grudg'd aught but a spiteful
    obeisance,   5
    Soon as a corpse outstretch'd starkly declar'd you a
    bride.
Come, speak truly to me ; what shameful rumour avouches
    Duty of years forsworn, honour in injury lost?

DOOR.

So be the tenant new, Caecilius, happy to own me,
    I'm not guilty, for all jealousy says it is I.   10
Never a fault was mine, nor man shall whisper it ever;
    Only, my friend, your mob's noisy " The door is a
    rogue."
Comes to the light some mischief, a deed uncivil arising,
    Loudly to me shout all, " Door, you are wholly to blame."

CATULLUS.

'Tis not enough so merely to say, so think to decide it. 15
    Better, who wills should feel, see it, who wills, to be
    true.

DOOR.

How then ? if here none asks, nor labours any to know it.

CATULLUS.

Nay, *I* ask it ; away scruple ; your hearer is I.

DOOR.

First, what rumour avers, they gave her to us a virgin—
    They lie on her. A light lady ! be sure, not alone   20
Clipp'd her an husband first ; weak stalk from a garden,
    a pointless
Falchion, a heart did ne'er fully to courage awake.
No ; to the son's own bed, 'tis said, that father ascended,
    Vilely ; with act impure stain'd the facinorous house.
Whether a blind fierce lust in his heart burnt sinfully
    flaming,   25
Or that inert that son's vigour, amort to delight,
Needed a sturdier arm, that franker quality somewhere,
    Looser of youth's fast-bound girdle, a virgin as yet.

CATULLUS.

Truly a noble father, a glorious act of affection !
    Thus in a son's kind sheets lewdly to puddle, his
    own.   30

DOOR.

Yet not alone of this, her crag Chinaean abiding
    Under, a watch-tower set warily, Brixia tells,
Brixia, trails whereby his waters Mella the golden,
    Mother of her, mine own city, Verona the fair.
Add Postumius yet, Cornelius also, a twice-told   35
    Folly, with whom our light mistress adultery knew.
Asks some questioner here " What? a door, yet privy to
    lewdness ?
You, from your owner's gate never a minute away ?
Strange to the talk o' the town ? since here, stout timber
    above you,
    Hung to the beam, you shut mutely or open again." 40
Many a shameful time I heard her stealthy profession,

While to the maids her guilt softly she hinted alone.
Spoke unabash'd her amours and named them singly, opining
Haply an ear to record fail'd me, a voice to reveal.
There was another; enough; his name I gladly dis-
  semble ;   . 45
Lest his lifted brows blush a disorderly rage.
Sir, 'twas a long lean suitor ; a process huge had assail'd
  him ;
'Twas for a pregnant womb falsely declar'd to be true.

LXVIII.

IF, when fortune's wrong with bitter misery whelms thee,
  Thou thy sad tear-scrawl'd letter, a mark to the
    storm,
Send'st, and bid'st me to succour a stranded seaman
  of Ocean,
    Toss'd in foam, from death's door to return thee
      again ;
Whom nor softly to rest love's tender sanctity
  suffers,   5
  Lost on a couch of lone slumber, unhappily lain ;
Nor with melody sweet of poets hoary the Muses
  Cheer, while worn with grief nightly the soul is
    awake :
Well-contented am I, that thou thy friendship avowest,
  Ask'st the delights of love from me, the pleasure of
    ⁸ hymns;   10
Yet lest all unnoted a kindred story bely thee,
  Deeming, Mallius, I calls of humanity shun ;
Hear what a grief is mine, what storm of destiny
  whelms me.
  Cease to demand of a soul's misery joy's sacrifice.

Once, what time white robes of manhood first did array
  me,   15
 Whiles in jollity life sported a spring holiday,
Youth ran riot enow; right well she knows me, the God-
  dess,
 She whose honey delights blend with a bitter annoy.
Henceforth dies sweet pleasure, in anguish lost of a
  brother's
 Funeral. O poor soul, brother, O heavily ta'en, 20
You all happier hours, you, dying brother, effaced;
 All our house lies low mournfully buried in you;
Quench'd untimely with you joy waits not ever a morrow,
 Joy which alive your love's bounty fed hour upon
  hour;
Now, since thou liest dead, heart-banish'd wholly desert
  me   25
 Vanities all, each gay freak of a riotous heart.

How then obey? You write 'Let not Verona, Catullus,
 Stay thee, if here each proud quality, Rome's emi-
  nence,
 Freely the light limbs warms thou leavest coldly to
  languish,'
 Infamy lies not there, Mallius, only regret. 30
So forgive me, if I, whom grief so rudely bereaveth,
 Deal not a joy myself know not, a beggar in all.
Books—if they're but scanty, a store full meagre, around
  me,
 Rome is alone my life's centre, a mansion of home,
Rome my abode, house, hearth; there wanes and
  waxes a life's span;   35
 Hither of all those choice cases attends me but one.
Therefore deem not thou aught spiteful bids me deny
  thee;

G

Say not 'his heart is false, haply, to jealousy leans,'
If nor books I send nor flatter sorrow to silence.
    Trust me, were either mine, either unask'd should
      appear.   40

GODDESSES, hide I may not in how great trial upheld
    me
    Allius, how no faint charities held me to life.
Nor shall time borne fleetly nor years' oblivion ever
    Make such zeal to the night fade, to the darkness,
    away.
As from me you learn it, of you shall many a thou-
    sand   45
    Learn it again.   Grow old, scroll, to declare it anew.

  . . . .
    . . . .
  . . . .
So to the dead increase honour in year upon year. 50
Nor to the spider, aloft her silk-slight flimsiness hang-
    ing,
    Allius aye unswept moulder, a memory dim.   (50)

Well you wot, how sore the deceit Amathusia wrought me,
    Well what a thing in love's treachery made me to fall;
Ready to burst in flame, as burn Trinacrian embers, 55
    Burn near Thermopylae's Oeta the fiery springs.
Sad, these piteous eyes did waste all wearily weeping, (55)
    Sad, these cheeks did rain ceaseless a showery woe.
Wakeful, as hill-born brook, which, afar off silvery
    gleaming,
    O'er his moss-grown crags leaps with a tumble a-
    down;   60
Brook which awhile headlong o'er steep and valley de-
    scending,

Crosses anon wide ways populous, hastes to the
    street ; (60)
Cheerer in heats o' the sun to the wanderer heavily
    fuming,
    Under a drought, when fields swelter agape to the
    sky.

Then as tossing shipmen amid black surges of Ocean, 65
    See some prosperous air gently to calm them arise,
Safe thro' Pollux' aid or Castor, alike entreated; (65)
    Mallius e'en such help brought me, a warder of harm.
He in a closed field gave scope of liberal entry;
    Gave me an house of love, gave me the lady
    within, 70
Busily there to renew love's even duty together;
    Thither afoot mine own mistress, a deity bright, (70)
Came, and planted firm her sole most sunny; beneath
    her
    Lightly the polish'd floor creak'd to the sandal again.

So with passion aflame came wistful Laodamia 75
    Into her husband's home, Protesilaus, of yore ;
Home o'er-lightly begun, ere slaughter'd victim aton-
    ing (75)
    Waited of heaven's high-thron'd company grace to
    agree.
Nought be to me so dear, O Maid Ramnusian, ever,
    I should against that law match me with opposite,
    I. 80
Bloodless of high sacrifice, how thirsts each desolate
    altar !
    This, when her husband fell, Laodamia did heed, (80)
Rapt from a bridegroom new, from his arms forced
    early to part her.
    Early; for hardly the first winter, another again,

Yet in many a night's long dream had sated her yearn-
  ing,   85
  So that love might wear cheerly, the master away ;
Which not long should abide, so presag'd surely the
  Parcae,   (85)
  If to the wars her lord hurry, for Ilion arm.

Now to revenge fair Helen, had Argos' chiefs, her puissance,
  Set them afield; for Troy rous'd them, a cry not of
    home,   90
  Troy, dark death universal, of Asia grave and Europe,
    Altar of heroes Troy, Troy of heroical acts,   (90)
Now to my own dear brother abhorred worker of
  ancient
  Death.   Ah woeful soul, brother, unhappily lost,
Ah fair light unblest, in darkness sadly receding,   95
 ' All our house lies low, brother, inearthed in you,
  Quench'd untimely with you, joy waits not ever a mor-
    row,   (95)
  Joy which alive your love's bounty fed hour upon
    hour.
Now on a distant shore, no kind mortality near him,
  Far all household love, every familiar urn,   100
Tomb'd in Troy the malign, in Troy the unholy reposing,
  Strangely the land's last verge holds him, a dungeon
    of earth.   (100)

Thither in haste all Greece, one armed people assembling,
  Flock'd on an ancient day, left the recesses of home,
  Lest in a safe content, unreach'd, his stolen adultress 105
  Paris inarm, in soft luxury quietly lain.

E'en such chance, fair queen, such misery, Laodamia, (105)
  Brought thee a loss as life precious, as heavenly
    breath,

Loss of a bridegroom dear; such whirling passion in
    eddies
    Suck'd thee adown, so drew sheer to a sudden
    abyss,   ·   110
Deep as Graian abyss near Pheneos o'er Cyllene, .
    Strainer of ooze impure milk'd from a watery fen; (110)
Hewn, so stories avouch, in a mountain's kernel; an hero
    Hew'd it, falsely declar'd Amphytrionian, he,
When those monster birds near grim Stymphalus his
    arrow   115
    Smote to the death ; such task bade him a dastardly
    lord.
So that another God might tread that portal of
    heaven   .   (115)
    Freely, nor Hebe fair wither a chaste eremite.
Yet than abyss more deep thy love, thy depth of
    emotion ;
    Love which school'd thy lord, made of a master a
    thrall.   120

Not to a grandsire old so priz'd, so lovely the grandson
    One dear daughter alone rears i' the soft of his
    years ;   (120)
He, long-wish'd for, an heir of wealth ancestral
    arriving,—
    Scarcely the tablets' marge holds him, a name to the
    will,
Straight all hopes laugh'd down, each baffled kinsman
    usurping   125
    Leaves to repose white hairs, stretches, a vulture,
    away ;
Not in her own fond mate so turtle snowy de-
    lighteth,   ·   (125)
    Tho' unabash'd, 'tis said, she the voluptuous hours

Snatches a thousand kisses, in amorous extasy biting.
  Yet, more lightly than all ranges a womanly will. 130
Great their love, their frenzy ; but all their frenzy before
    thee ˙
    Fail'd, once clasp'd thy lord splendid in aureat
      hair.   (130)

Worthy in all or part thee, Laodamia, to rival,
  Sought me my own sweet love, journey'd awhile to
    my arms.
Round her playing oft ran Cupid thither or hither, 135
  Lustrous, array'd in bright broidery, saffron of hue.
What, to Catullus alone if a wayward fancy resort not ?
  Must I pale for a stray frailty, the shame of an
    hour ?   -   (136)
Nay ; lest all too much such jealous folly provoke her.
  Juno's self, a supreme glory celestial, oft   140
Crushes her eager rage, in wedlock-injury flaring,
  Knowing yet right well Jove, what a losel is he. (140)

Yet, for a man with Gods shall never lawfully match
    him

  . . . .
. . . .   145
  . . . .
. . . .
. . . .
    150
. . . .
  . . . .
. . . .
  . . . .
. . . .   155
  . . . .

. . . .
. . . .
. . . .
. . . .   160
. . . .

Lift thy father, a weak burden, unholpen, abhorr'd.
Not that a father's hand my love led to me, nor odours
   Wafted her home on rich airs, of Assyria born ;
Stealthy the gifts she gave me, a night unspeakable
   o'er us,   165 (145)
   Gifts from her husband's dreams verily stolen, his
   own.
Then 'tis enough for me, if mine, mine only remaineth
   That one day, whose stone shines with an happier
   hue.

So, it is all I can, take, Allius, answer, a little
   Verse to requite thy much friendship, a contrary
   boon.   170 (150)
So your household names no rust nor seamy defacing
   Soil this day, that new morrow, the next to the last.
Gifts full many to these heaven send as largely
   requiting,
   Gifts Themis ever wont deal to the pious of yore.
Joys come plenty to thee, to thy own fair lady
   together,   175 (155)
   Come to that house of mirth, come to the lady within ;
Joy to the forward friend, our love's first fashioner,
   Anser,
   Author of all this fair history, founder of all.
Lastly beyond them, above them, on her more lovely
   than even
   Life, my lady, for whose life it is happy to be. 180 (160)

LXIX.

RUFUS, it is no wonder if yet no woman assenting
  Softly to thine embrace tender a delicate arm.
Not tho' a gift should seek, some robe most filmy, to
    move her ;
  Not for a cherish'd gem's clarity, lucid of hue.

Deep in a valley, thy arms, such evil story maligns
    thee,   5
  Rufus, a villain goat houses, a grim denizen.
All are afraid of it, all ; what wonder? a rascally crea-
    ture,
  Verily ! not with such company dally the fair.

Slay, nor pity the brute, our nostril's rueful aversion.
  Else admire not if each ravisher angrily fly.   10

LXX.

SAITH my lady to me, no man shall wed me, but
    only
  Thou ; no other if e'en Jove should approach me
    to woo ;
Yea ; but a woman's words, when a lover fondly
    desireth,
  Limn them on ebbing floods, write on a wintery
    gale.

LXXII.

LESBIA, thou didst swear thou knewest only Catullus,
  Cared'st not, if him thine arms chained, a Jove to
    retain.

Then not alone I loved thee, as each light lover a
    mistress,
    Lov'd as a father his own sons, or an heir to the
    name.
Now I know thee aright ; so, if more hotly desiring,   5
    Yet must count thee a soul cheaper, a frailty to scorn.
'Friend,' thou say'st, 'you cannot.' Alas ! such injury
    leaveth
    Blindly to doat poor love's folly, malignly to will.

LXXIII.

NEVER again think any to work aught kindly soever,
    Dream that in any abides honour, of injury free.
Love is a debt in arrear; time's parted service avails
    not ;
    Rather is only the more sorrow, a heavier ill :
Chiefly to me, whom none so fierce, so deadly deceiv-
    ing   5
    Troubleth, as he whose friend only but inly was I.

LXXIV.

GELLIUS heard that his uncle in ire exploded, if any
    Dared, some wanton, a fault practise, a levity speak.
Not to be slain himself, see Gellius handle his uncle's
    Lady ; no Harpocrates muter, his uncle is hush'd.
So what he aim'd at, arriv'd at, anon let Gellius e'en
    this   5
    Uncle abuse ; not a word yet will his uncle assay.

LXXVIII.

BROTHERS twain has Gallus, of whom one owns a delightful
  Son ; his brother a fair lady, delightfuller yet.
Gallant sure is Gallus, a pair so dainty uniting ;
  Lovely the lady, the lad lovely, a company sweet.
Foolish sure is Gallus, an o'er-incurious husband ;   5
  Uncle, a wife once taught luxury, stops not at one.

LXXIX.

LESBIUS, handsome is he. Why not ? if Lesbia loves him
  Far above all your tribe, angry Catullus, or you.
Only let all your tribe sell off, and follow, Catullus,
  Kiss but his handsome lips children, a plenary three.

LXXXI.

WHAT ? not in all this city, Juventius, ever a gallant
  Poorly to win love's fresh favour of amorous you,
Only the lack-love signor, a wretch from sickly Pisaurum,
  Guest of your hearth, no gilt statue as ashy as he ?
Now your very delight, whose faithless fancy Catullus   5
  Banisheth.   Ah light-reck'd lightness, apostasy vile !

LXXXII.

WOULDST thou, Quintius, have me a debtor ready to owe thee
  Eyes, or if earth have joy goodlier any than eyes?
One thing take not from me, to me more goodly than even
  Eyes, or if earth have joy goodlier any than eyes.

LXXXIII.

LESBIA while her lord stands near, rails ever upon me.
  This to the fond weak fool seemeth a mighty delight.
Dolt, you see not at all. Could she forget me, to rail not,
  Nought were amiss ; if now scold she, or if she revile,
'Tis not alone to remember ; a shrewder stimulus arms
    her,   5
  Anger ; her heart doth burn verily, thus to revile.

LXXXIV.

Stipends Arrius ever on opportunity *shtipends*,
  Ambush as *hambush* still Arrius used to declaim.
Then, hoped fondly the words were a marvel of articula-
    tion,
  While with an *h* immense '*hambush*' arose from his
    heart.
So his mother of old, so e'en spoke Liber his uncle,   5
  Credibly ; so grandsire, grandam alike did agree.

Syria took him away ; all ears had rest for a moment ;
  Lightly the lips those words, slightly could utter again.
None was afraid any more of a sound so clumsy
    returning ;
  Sudden a solemn fright seized us, a message arrives. 10
' News from Ionia country ; the sea, since Arrius enter'd,
  Changed ; 'twas *Ionian* once, now 'twas *Hionian* all.'

LXXXV.

HALF I hate, half love. How so? one haply requireth.
  Nay, I know not ; alas feel it, in agony groan.

LXXXVI.

LOVELY to many a man is Quintia ; shapely, majestic,
    Stately, to me ; each point singly 'tis easy to grant.
'Lovely' the whole, I grant not ; in all that bodily
        largeness,
    Lives not a grain of salt, breathes not a charm any-
        where.
Lesbia—she is lovely, an even temper of utmost   5
    Beauty, that every charm stealeth of every fair.

LXXXVII & LXXV.

NE'ER shall woman avouch herself so rightly beloved,
    Friend, as rightly thou art, Lesbia, lovely to me.
Ne'er was a bond so firm, no troth so faithfully
        plighted,
    Such as against our love's venture in honour am I.

Now so sadly my heart, dear Lesbia, draws me asunder, 5
    So in her own misspent worship uneasily lost,
Wert thou blameless in all, I may not longer approve
        thee,
    Do anything thou wilt, cannot an enemy be.

LXXVI.

IF to a man bring joy past service dearly remember'd,
    'When to the soul her thought speaks, to be blameless
        of ill ;
Faith not rudely profan'd, nor in oath or charter abused
    Heaven, a God's mis-sworn sanctity, deadly to men.

Then doth a life-long pleasure await thee surely,
    Catullus, 5
Pleasure of all this love's traitorous injury born.

Whatso a man may speak, whom charity leads to another,
    Whatso enact, by me spoken or acted is all.
Waste on a traitorous heart, nor finding kindly requital.
    Therefore cease, nor still bleed agoniz'd any more. 10

Make thee as iron a soul, thyself draw back from affliction.
    Yea, tho' a God say nay, be not unhappy for aye.
What? it is hard long love so lightly to leave in a
    moment?
Hard; yet abides this one duty, to do it: obey.
Here lies safety alone, one victory must not fail
    thee. 15
One last stake to be lost haply, perhaps to be won.

O great Gods immortal, if you can pity or ever
    Lighted above dark death's shadow, a help to the
    lost;
Ah! look, a wretch, on me; if white and blameless in
    all I
Liv'd, then take this long canker of anguish away. 20
If to my inmost veins, like dull death drowsily
    creeping,
Every delight, all heart's pleasure it wholly benumbs.

Not anymore I pray for a love so faulty returning,
    Not that a wanton abide chastely, she may not again.
Only for health I ask, a disease so deadly to banish. 25
    Gods vouchsafe it, as I ask, that am harmless of ill.

LXXVII.

RUFUS, a friend so vainly believ'd, so wrongly relied in,
  (Vainly? alas the reward fail'd not, a heavier ill;)
Could'st thou thus steal on me, a lurking viper, an aching
    Fire to the bones, nor leave aught to delight any more?
Nought to delight any more! ah cruel poison of equal 5
  Lives! ah breasts that grew each to the other awhile!
Yet far most this grieves me, to think thy slaver abhorred
    Foully my own love's lips soileth, a purity rare.
Thou shalt surely atone thine injury: centuries harken,
  Know thee afar; grow old, fame, to declare him anew. 10

LXXXVIII.

GELLIUS, how if a man in lust with a mother, a sister
  Rioteth, one uncheck'd night, to iniquity bare?
How if a man's dark passion an aunt's own chastity spare not?
    Canst thou tell what vast infamy lieth on him?

Infamy lieth on him, no farthest Tethys, or ancient 5
  Ocean, of hundred streams father, abolisheth yet.
Infamy none o'ersteps, nor ventures any beyond it.
    Not tho' a scorpion heat melt him, his own paramour.

LXXXIX.

GELLIUS—he's full meagre. It is no wonder, a friendly
  Mother, a sister is his loveable, healthy withal.

Then so friendly an uncle, a world of pretty relations.
Must not a man so blest meagre abide to the last?
Yea, let his hand touch only what hands touch only to
    trespass ;   5
Reason enough to become meagre, enough to remain.

XC.

RISE from a mother's shame with Gellius hatefully
    wedded,
One to be taught gross rites Persic, a Magian he.
Weds with a mother a son, so needs should a Magian
    issue,
Save in her evil creed Persia determineth ill.
Then shall a son, so born, chant down high favour of
    heaven,   5
Melting lapt in flame fatly the slippery caul.

XCI.

THINK not a hope so false rose, Gellius, in me to find thee
    Faithful in all this love's anguish ineffable yet,
For that in heart I knew thee, had in thee honour
    imagin'd,
    Held thee a soul to abhor vileness or any reproach.

Only in her, I knew, thou found'st not a mother, a sister, 5
    Her that awhile for love wearily made me to pine.
Yea tho' mutual use did bind us straitly together,
    Scarcely methought could lie cause to desert me
    therein.

Thou found'st reason enow ; so joys thy spirit in every
    Shame, wherever is aught heinous, of infamy born. 10

XCII.

LESBIA doth but rail, rail ever upon me, nor endeth
    Ever.   A life I stake, Lesbia loves me at heart.
Ask me a sign? Our score runs parallel. I that abuse
    her
    Ever, a life to the stake, Lesbia, love thee at heart.

XCIII.

LIGHTLY methinks I reck if Cæsar smile not upon me :
    Care not, whether a white, whether a swarth-skin, is he.

XCIV.

MENTULA—wanton is he; his calling sure is a wanton's.
    Herbs to the pot, 'tis said wisely, the name to the man.

XCV.

NINE times winter had end, nine times flush'd summer in
    harvest,
    Ere to the world gave forth Cinna, the labour of years,
Zmyrna ; but in one month Hortensius hundred on
    hundred
    Verses, an unripe birth feeble, of hurry begot.

Zmyrna to far Satrachus, to the stream of Cyprus,
    ascendeth ;   5
    Zmyrna with eyes unborn study the centuries hoar.
Padus her own ill child shall bury, Volusius' annals ;
    In them a mackerel oft house him, a wrapper of ease.

Dear to my heart be a friend's unbulky memorial ever ;
    Cherish an Antimachus, weighty as empty, the mob. 10

XCVI.

IF to the silent dead aught sweet or tender ariseth,
    Calvus, of our dim grief's common humanity born ;
When to a love long cold some pensive pity recals us,
    When for a friend long lost wakes some unhappy regret ;
Not so deeply, be sure, Quintilia's early departing   5
    Grieves her, as in thy love dureth a plenary joy.

XCVIII.

ASKS some booby rebuke, some prolix prattler a judgment ?
    Vettius, all were said verily truer of you.
Tongue so noisome as yours, come chance, might surely
    on order
    Bend to the mire, or lick dirt from a beggarly shoe.
Would you on all of us, all, bring, Vettius, utterly ruin ? 5
    Speak ; not a doubt, 'twill come utterly, ruin on all.

XCIX.

DEAR one, a kiss I stole, while you did wanton a-playing,
    Sweet ambrosia, love, never as honily sweet.

Dearly the deed I paid for ; an hour's long misery waning
    Ended, as I agoniz'd hung to the point of a cross,
    Hoping vain purgation ; alas ! no potion of any   5
    Tears could abate that fair angriness, youthful as you.

Hardly the sin was in act, your lips did many a falling
    Drop dilute, which anon every finger away
Cleansed apace, lest still my mouth's infection abiding
    Stain, like slaver abhorr'd breath'd from a foul frica-
        trice.   10

Add, that a booty to love in misery me to deliver
    You did spare not, a fell worker of all agonies,
So that, again transmuted, a kiss ambrosia seeming
    Sugary, turn'd to the strange harshness of harsh
      hellebore.

Then such dolorous end since your poor lover awaiteth, 15
    Never a kiss will I venture, a theft any more.

C.

QUINTIUS, AUFILENA ; to Caelius, Aufilenus ;
    Lovers each, fair flower either of youths Veronese.
One to the brother bends, and one to the sister.   A noble
    Friendship, if e'er was true friendship, a rare brother-
      hood.

Ask me to which I lean? You, Caelius: yours a devotion 5
    Single, a faith of tried quality, steady to me ;
Into my inmost veins when love sank fiercely to burn
    them.
    Mighty be your bright love, Caelius, happy be you !

CI.

BORNE o'er many a land, o'er many a level of ocean,
    Here to the grave I come, brother, of holy repose,
  Sadly the last poor gifts, death's simple duty, to bring
    thee ;
    Unto the silent dust vainly to murmur a cry.

Since thy form deep-shrouded an evil destiny taketh   5
    From me, O hapless ghost, brother, O heavily ta'en,

Yet this bounty the while, these gifts ancestral of usance
  Homely, the sad slight store piety grants to the tomb;
Drench'd in a brother's tears, and weeping freshly,
    receive them ;
  Yea, take, brother, a long Ave, a timeless adieu.   10

CII.

IF to a friend sincere, Cornelius, e'er was a secret
  Trusted, a friend whose soul steady to honour abides ;
Me to the same brotherhood doubt not to be inly devoted,
  Sworn upon oath, to the last secret, an Harpocrates.

CIII.

BRIEFLY, the sesterces all, give back, full quantity, Silo,
  Then be a bully beyond exorability, you :
Else, if money be all, O cease so lewdly to practise
  Bawd, yet bully beyond exorability, you.

CIV.

WHAT? should a lover adore, yet cruelly slander adoring?
  I my lady, than eyes goodlier easily she ?
Nay, I rail not at all. How rail, so blindly desiring?
  Tappo alone dare brave all that is heinous, or you.

CV.

MENTULA toils, Pimplea, the Muses' mountain, ascend-
    ing:
  They with pitchforks hurl Mentula dizzily down.

CVI.

WALKS with a salesman a beauty, your eyes that beauty
  discerning ?
  Doubt not your eyes speak true ; Sir, 'tis a beauty to
  sell.

CVII.

IF to delight man's wish, joy e'er unlook'd for, unhop'd for,
  Falleth, a joy were such proper, a bliss to the soul.
Then 'tis a joy to the soul, like gold of Lydia precious,
  Lesbia mine, that thou com'st to delight me again.

Com'st yet again long-hop'd, long-look'd for vainly, re-
  turnest   5
  Freely to me.   O day white with a luckier hue !
Lives there happier any than I, I only ? a fairer
  Destiny ?   Life so sweet know ye, or aught parallel ?

CVIII.

LOATHLY Cominius, if e'er this people's voice should
  arraign thee,
  Hoary with all unclean infamy, worthy to die ;
First should a tongue, I doubt not, of old so deadly to
  goodness,
  Fall extruded, of each vulture a hungry regale ;
Gouged be the carrion eyes some crow's black maw to
  replenish,   5
  Stomach a dog's fierce teeth harry, a wolf the remains.

CIX.

THINK you truly, belov'd, this bond of duty between us,
  Lasteth, an ever-new jollity, ne'er to decease?
Grant it, Gods immortal, assure her promise in earnest;
  Yea, be the lips sincere; yea, be the words from her
    heart.
So still rightly remain our lovers' charter, a life-long   5
  Friendship in us, whose faith fades not away to the last.

CX.

AUFILENA, the fair, if kind, is a favourite ever;
  Asks she a price, then yields frankly? the price is her
    own.
You, that agreed to be kind, now vilely the treaty dis-
    honour,
  Give not at all, nor again take;—'tis a wrong to a
    wrong.

Not to deceive were noble, a chastity ne'er had
    assented,   5
  Aufilena; but you—blindly to grasp at a gain,
Yet to withhold the effects,—'tis a greed more loathly
    than harlot's
  Vileness, a wretch whose limbs ply to the lusts of a
    town.

CXI.

ONE lord only to love, one, Aufilena, to live for,
  Praise can a bride nowhere goodlier any betide;
Yet, when a niece with an uncle is even mother or even
  Cousin—of all paramours this were as heinous as all.

CXII.

NASO, if you show much, your company shows but a very
    Little ; a man you show, Naso, a woman in one.

CXIII.

POMPEY the first time consul, as yet Maecilia counted
    Two paramours ; reappears Pompey a consul again,
Two still, Cinna, remain ; but grown, each unit an even
    Thousand.   Truly the stock's fruitful : adultery breeds.

CXIV.

RIGHTLY a lordly demesne makes Firman Mentula count
    for
Wealthy ! the rich fine things, then the variety there !
Game in plenty to choose, fish, field, and meadow with
    hunting ;
    Only the waste exceeds strangely the quantity still.
Wealthy? perhaps I grant it ; if all, wealth asks for, is
    absent.   5
    Praise the demesne ? no doubt ; only be needy the man.

CXV.

ACRES thirty in all, good grass, own Mentula master ;
    Forty to plough ; bare seas, arid or empty, the rest.
    Poorly methinks might Croesus a man so sumptuous
        equal,
    Counted in one rich park owner of all he can ask.

Grass or plough, big woods, much mountain, mighty
    morasses ;   5
On to the farthest North, on to the boundary main.

Vastness is all that is here ; yet Mentula reaches a vaster—
Man? not so ; 'tis a vast mountainous ominous He.

CXVI.

OFT with a studious heart, which hunted closely, requiring
    Skill great Battiades' poesies haply to send,
Laying thus thy rage in rest, lest everlasting
    Darts should reach me, to wound still an assailable
    head :

Barren now I see that labour of any requital,   5
    Gellius ; here all prayers fall to the ground, nor avail.
No ; but a robe I carry, the barbs, thy folly, to muffle ;
    Mine strike sure ; thy deep injury *they* shall atone.

FRAGMENTS.

II.

Here I give to be thine a fair grove, an holy, Priapus,
Where thy Lampsacus holds thee in chamber seemly,
    Priapus ;   .
God, in every city, thou, most ador'd on a sea-shore
Hellespontian, eminent most of oystery sea-shores.

IV.

Rapidly the spirit in an agony fled away.

V.

Where yon lucent mast-top, a cup of silver, arises.

NOTES.

VIII. 2.

Lost is the lost, thou know'st it, and the past is past.

I am indebted for this expression to a translation of this poem by Dr. J. A. Symonds, the whole of which I should have quoted here, had it not been unfortunately mislaid.

XIV. 20.

Plague-prodigy.

Proves a plague-prodigy to God and man.
> BROWNING, *Ring and Book*, v. 664.

XVII. 26.

Rondel.

The round plate of iron which, according to Rich, Companion to the Latin Dictionary, p. 609, formed the lower part of the sock worn by horses, mules, &c., when on a journey, and, unlike our horse-shoes, was removable at the end of it.

XXII. 11.

Looby

a clown.

> Let me now the vices trace,
> From his father's scoundrel race.
> What could give the looby such airs ?
> Were they masons ? were they butchers ?
> >   TICKELL, *Theristes or the Lordling*, 23-26.

XXIII.

For a spirited, though coarse, version of this poem, see Cotton's Poems, p. 608, ed. 1689.

6   *Lathy.*

> On a lathy horse, all legs and length.
> >   BROWNING, *Flight of the Duchess*, v. 21.

XXIX. 8.

The connexion between Adonis and the dove is specially referred to by Diogenianus (*Praef.* p. 180 in Leutsch and Schneidewin's *Paroemiographi Graeci*). It formed part of the legends of Cyprus, and was alluded to by the lyric poet Timocreon (*Bergk. Poetae Lyrici Graeci*, p. 1203). Compare Browning :—

> Pompilia was no pigeon, Venus' Pet.
> >   *Ring and Book*, v. 701.

XXXV. 7.

So he'll quickly devour the way,

move quickly over the road. So Shakespeare :

> > Starting so
> He seem'd in running to devour the way,
> Staying no longer question.
> >   *2nd Part of Henry IV.*, Act i. sc. I.

XXXVII. 10.

With scorpion I, with emblem all your haunt will scrawl.

A member of the Saraceni family at Vicenza, finding that a beautiful widow did not favour him, scribbled filthy pictures over the door.   The affair was brought before the Council of Ten at Venice.

TROLLOPE'S *Paul the Pope*, p. 158.

XLIII. 3.

Mouth scarce tenible,

easily running over.

XLV. 7.

A sulky lion.

Properly "green-eyed."   The epithet would seem to be not merely picturesque; the glaring of the eyes would be more marked in proportion as the beast was in a fiercer and more excitable state.

LI. 5—12.

I watch thy grace; and in its place
My heart a charmed slumber keeps,
    While I muse upon thy face;
And a languid fire creeps
    Thro' my veins to all my frame,
Dissolvingly and slowly: soon
    From thy rose-red lips my name
Floweth; and then, as in a swoon,
    With dinning sound my ears are rife,
My tremulous tongue faltereth,

I lose my colour, I lose my breath,
I drink the cup of a costly death,
Brimmed with delicious draughts of warmest life.
                                    TENNYSON, *Eleänore.*

LIV. 6.

Yet thou flee'st not above my keen iambics.

This line is quoted as Catullus's by Porphyrion on Hor. c. I. 16, 24. His words, *Catullus cum maledicta minaretur,* compared with the last lines of this poem, *Irascere iterum meis iambis Inmerentibus, unice imperator,* seem to justify my view that they belong here. See my large edition, p. 217, fragm. I. The following line, *So may destiny, &c.,* is a supplement of my own: it forms a natural introduction to the *Si non uellem* of v. 10.

LV.

This is the only instance where Catullus has introduced a spondee into the second foot of the phalaecian, which then becomes decasyllabic. The alternation of this decasyllabic rhythm with the ordinary hendecasyllable is studiously artistic; I have retained it throughout. In the series of dactylic lines 17—22, Catullus no doubt intended to convey the idea of rapidity, as, in the spondaic line immediately following, of labour.

4   *You on Circus, in all the bills but you, Sir.*

There seems to be no authority for the meaning ordinarily assigned to *libellis,* "book-shops." I prefer to explain the word placards, either announcing the sale of Camerius's effects, which would imply that he was in debt, or describing him as a lost article.

LXI.

In the rhythm of this poem, I have been obliged to deviate in two points from Catullus. (1) In him the first foot of each line is nearly always a trochee, only rarely a spondee : the monotonous effect of a positional trochee in English, to say nothing of the difficulty, induced me to substitute a spondee more frequently. (2) I have been rather less scrupulous in allowing the last foot of the glyconic lines to be a dactyl (-◡◡), in place of the more correct cretic (-◡-).

108.   The words in italics are a supplement of my own.

LXII. 39—61.

Look in a garden croft, when a flower privily growing, &c.

Opinion.   Look how a flower that close in closes grows,
Hid from rude cattle, bruised with no ploughs,
Which th' air doth stroke, sun strengthen, showers shoot higher,
It many youths and many maids desire ;
The same, when cropt by cruel hand 'tis wither'd,
No youths at all, no maidens have desired ;
So a virgin while untouch'd she doth remain
Is dear to hers ; but when with body's stain
Her chaster flower is lost, she leaves to appear
Or sweet to young men or to maidens dear.

Truth.   Virgins, O Virgins, to sweet Hymen yield,
For as a lone vine in a naked field
Never extols her branches, never bears
Ripe grapes, but with a headlong heaviness wears
Her tender body, and her highest sprout
Is quickly levell'd with her fading root ;

By whom no husbandmen, no youths will dwell ;
But if by fortune she be married well,
To the elm her husband, many husbandmen
And many youths inhabit by her then ;
So whilst a virgin doth untouch'd abide,
All unmanur'd she grows old with her pride ;
But when to equal wedlock, in fit time,
Her fortune and endeavour lets her climb,
Dear to her love and parents she is held.
Virgins, O Virgins, to sweet Hymen yield.

BEN JONSON, The Barriers.

LXIII.

In the metre of this poem Catullus observes the following
general type—

$$\overline{\cup\cup}\acute{-} \quad \cup\,\bar{-}\,\underset{\cup\,\cup}{} \quad \bar{-}\cup \;\; — \quad \| \quad \overline{\cup\cup}\acute{-} \quad \cup\overline{\cup\cup} \quad \underset{\cup\cup}{\cup\bar{-}} \quad \text{(so Heyse.)}$$

Except in 18, *Hilarate aere citatis erroribus animum*, 53, *Et
earum omnia adirem furibunda latibula*, where the Ionic a
minore, which seems to have been the original basis of the
rhythm, is preserved intact in the former half of the line.   I
have followed Catullus generally with exactness, but with an
occasional resolution of one long into two short syllables, where
it has not been introduced by the poet, *e. g.* in 31, 34, 49, 64,
65, 68, 79.   In v. 10 I have ventured on a license which
Catullus does not admit, but which is, I think, justified by
other and earlier specimens of the metre, an anaclasis of the
original Ionic a minore at the end of the line.   In reading this
poem it should never be forgotten that there is a pause in the
middle of each line, which practically divides it into two halves.
Tennyson, in his *Boadicea*, written on the model of the *Attis*,
divides each verse similarly in the middle ; but in the first half
he has changed the rhythm of Catullus to a trochaic rhythm, in

the second, while producing much of the effect of the *Attis* by the accumulation of short syllables at the end of the line, he has not bound himself to the same strictly defined feet as Catullus, and generally has preferred to take from the somewhat emasculate character of the verse by adding an unaccented syllable at the close.

LXIII.

8   *Taborine*

Beat loud the tabourines, let the trumpets blow.
> *Troilus and Cressida*, Act iv. sc. 5.

16   *Aby*

abide ; as, I think, in Spenser's *Faerie Queene*, vi. 2, 19.

> But he was fierce and whot,
> Ne time would give, nor any termes aby.

Below, lxiv. 297, I have used it in its more common meaning of atoning for, *Faerie Queene*, iv. 1, 53.

> Yet thou, false Squire, his fault shalt deare aby,
> And with thy punishment his penance shalt supply.

Midsummer Night's Dream, iii. 2.

> Lest to thy peril thou aby it dear.

24   *Ululation.*

> There sighs, complaints, and ululations loud
> Resounded through the air without a star.
> > LONGFELLOW'S *Dante Inf.* iii. 22.

I

41 *When he smote the shadowy twilight with his healthy team sublime.*

> Ere yet they blind the stars, and the wild team
> Which love thee, yearning for thy yoke, arise,
> And shake the darkness from their loosen'd manes,
> And beat the twilight into flakes of fire.
> > TENNYSON, *Tithonus.*

83 *On a nervy neck.*

> > Four maned lions hale
> The sluggish wheels ; solemn their toothed maws,
> Their surly eyes brow-hidden, heavy paws
> Uplifted drowsily, and nervy tails
> Covering their tawny brushes.
> > KEATS, *Endymion*, II. ad fin.

LXIV. 160.

Yet to your household thou, your kindred palaces olden.

I have combined *thou* with *your* purposely, to suggest the idea conveyed in *uestras* as opposed to *potuisti*, the family abode as opposed to the individual Theseus.

183 *Flexibly fleeting*

bent as they move rapidly through the water.

186 *No glimmer of hope*

from Heyse,

Keinerlei Flucht, kein Schimmer der Hoffnung, stumm liegt Alles.

258 *Gordian.*

She was a gordian shape of dazzling hue,
Vermilion-spotted, golden, green, and blue.
KEATS, *Lamia*, Part I.

308 *Wreaths sat on each hoar crown, whose snows flush'd rosy beneath them.*

I have attempted here to give what I conceive Catullus may
have meant to convey by the remarkable collocation *At roseo
niueae residebant uertice uittae.* Properly, the wreaths are rosy,
the locks snow-white ; but the colour of the wreaths is so blent
with the colour of the locks that each is lost in the other, and an
inversion of epithets becomes possible.

So, in fury of heart, shall death's stern reaper, Achilles.

A verse seems to have been lost here, which I have thus
supplied.

LXVIII. 149.

*So, it is all I can, take, Allius, answer, a little
Verse, to requite thy much friendship, a contrary boon.*

These little rites, a stone, a verse, receive,
'Tis all a father, all a friend can give.
POPE, *Epitaph on the children of Lord Digby.*

LXIX. 4.

Clarity

clearness, transparency.

Here clarity of candour, history's soul,
The critical mind in short.
BROWNING, *Ring and Book*, i. 925.

LXX.

Sir Philip Sidney thus translates this poem :—

Unto no body my woman saith shee had rather a wife be,
  Then.to myself, not though Jove grew a suter of hers.
These he her words, but a woman's words to a love that is
    eager,
  Midde [windes ?] or waters stream do require to be writ.

XCIX. 10.

Fricatrice.

To a lewd harlot, a base fricatrice.
                    BEN JONSON, *The Fox*, iv. 2.

THE END.

BRADBURY, EVANS, AND CO., PRINTERS, WHITEFRIARS.